The Streets Stained My Soul 3

Lock Down Publications and Ca$h
Presents
The Streets Stained My Soul 3
A Novel by *Marcellus Allen*

Lock Down Publications
P.O. Box 944
Stockbridge, Ga 30281

Copyright 2022 by Marcellus Allen
The Streets Stained My Soul 3

First Edition January 2022
Printed in the United States of America

This is a work of fiction. Names, characters, places, and incidents either are products of the author's imagination or are used fictitiously. Any similarity to actual events or locales or persons, living or dead, is entirely coincidental.

Lock Down Publications
Like our page on Facebook: Lock Down Publications @
www.facebook.com/lockdownpublications.ldp
Book interior design by: **Shawn Walker**
Edited by: **Shamika Smith**

Stay Connected with Us!

Text **LOCKDOWN** to 22828 to stay up-to-date with new releases, sneak peaks, contests and more...

Thank you!

Submission Guideline.

Submit the first three chapters of your completed manuscript to ldpsubmissions@gmail.com, subject line: Your book's title. The manuscript must be in a .doc file and sent as an attachment. Document should be in Times New Roman, double spaced and in size 12 font. Also, provide your synopsis and full contact information. If sending multiple submissions, they must each be in a separate email.

Have a story but no way to send it electronically? You can still submit to LDP/Ca$h Presents. Send in the first three chapters, written or typed, of your completed manuscript to:

LDP: Submissions Dept
P.O. Box 944
Stockbridge, Ga 30281

DO NOT send original manuscript. Must be a duplicate.

Provide your synopsis and a cover letter containing your full contact information.

Thanks for considering LDP and Ca$h Presents

Marcellus Allen

Chapter 1
Freeze

"Good, baby, I can't believe how smart you've gotten since I've been gone. Keep it up, and you'll end up being a doctor or something. Insha Allah!" I told my daughter, Aaliyah.

We were sitting in her room going over her math homework. I stared at her for a few seconds and was still in awe at how much she looked like her mother. *Damn, she's growing up.* She was only a year old when I was captured and had to give them crackers a decade of my life. I had to help raise her over the phone, but it was worth it because we had an unbreakable bond.

"Daddy, I told you I wanna be a fashion designer." She looked up at me like her mother did when her mind couldn't be changed.

"If that's Allah's will, then it shall pass," I replied, not seeing the point in arguing with her. I'd only been home for a lil over a week and didn't wanna force my will on her. I knew from experience that the more a father tried to enforce his will on his daughter, the harder she would rebel. I heard the doorbell start to ring, then left the room, already knowing who it was.

"Lonzo! Brother Raheem is here," my wife, Fatimah, called out.

When I walked into the living room, they were standing by the couch, waiting on me before they sat down. My beautiful wife had her whole body wrapped up, everything except her head.

A woman of Islam wasn't required to cover her face inside the house, and I wasn't insecure enough to force her.

"Brother Raheem, As-Salam Alaikum," I greeted my brother in faith with a handshake.

"Wa-Alaikum-as-salaam?"

We all sat down and got comfortable for what we knew would be a long conversation. Brother Raheem was the Imam of the Mosque that my wife had been attending while I was gone. Once I finally submitted to Allah's will in prison, Fatimah immediately did the same on the outside. Without a doubt, Islam saved our relationship and gave her a deeper purpose. We got married right after and, for the most part, we didn't have any problems. Her only demand was that I leave the streetz in the past and make her, my daughter, and Islam the future. I gave her my word.

"Brother Zo, as you know, your wife and daughter have become pillars at the Mosque and a great benefit to the elderly and widows. Now that you are home, the home cycle is complete. Allah Akbar."

"Allah Akbar," I replied.

"All of the brothers want the best for you, and we are prepared to help you in any capacity that we can," he vowed.

"Thank you, Imam. I'm fully committed to Allah and my wife; nothing else matters." I held Fatimah's hand.

"Good, my brother," He nodded along with a genuine smile on his face. Then it disappeared as fast as it came while his eyes became smaller and darker. "Brother Zo, I have to ask for the safety of the Mosque. It's my duty, so don't take it personally."

"I nodded. Go ahead, brother."

"Have you completely put the street life behind you and are strictly on the path of Islam? It is solely Allah who judges men. I only ask because it is my sacred duty to protect the Mosque from all dangers." He peered into my eyes, doing his best to read my soul.

I could feel my wife staring at me, burning a hole in my face. She'd made it more than clear that if I ever got back into the streets that she would leave me with no questions asked. That was our agreement. That was right after I submitted to Allah and our relationship needed saving. But all that was before they killed Top-gun. They had to pay for that. I felt the anger boiling my blood and knew my eyes would betray my demons to the Imam, so I quickly thought of my daughter and how much I loved her before I responded.

"They're completely behind me, and my heart only has room for the things that Allah deems permissible," I lied. I had to block the sight of the two people I'd left slumped in the car. The woman, Naughty, had begged for her and her unborn child's life to be spared. I couldn't afford to leave a witness.

It weighed heavy on my heart that I killed two innocent people. I really thought that it was Juice sitting behind the wheel. Trey had given me bad intel, and I was still having thoughts of killin' him. I prayed Allah would forgive me. "I only wanna serve Allah and make my wife more than happy. If there's anything I can do to help serve the brothers, just let me know, Imam!!"

Allah Akhbar," Imam Raheem proclaimed with a smile on his face. "There is something that we think you will be perfect for, Insha Allah. I know you plan on helping your wife take y'alls real estate company to the next level, and I pray Allah pours his blessings on it. However, we're starting up a youth mentor program, and we hope Allah puts it on your heart to take an active role in it. We need brothers like you."

"I'll pray to Allah about it." My wife squeezed my hand to let me know how she felt. I knew soon as he said it that she wanted me to do it.

They probably planned this. "I don't want to commit to something so big without praying first and giving it much thought," I replied.

"Wise man." He nodded in agreement. "I pray Allah shows you his will when you do. Every day a new child becomes a gangbanger or a dope dealer or even both. We're losing the battle to the prison system, and it's not even close. We can't reach the youth, and I know why. It's because most of the elders are out of touch with the times and stuck in our ways. I sincerely believe that brothers like you can more than reach the youth. You can change and save lives."

"Brothers like me?" I raised my eyebrows.

"No disrespect, brother. But yeah, like you." He sat up on the edge of the couch. "Brothers that have lived that life and still found their way back to Allah. Brothers that have walked through the fire and Allah showed how merciful he is by pulling you out. I've never come close to living that life, Allah Akhbar, but at the same time, it prevents me from being able to relate to the new generation. This is the same problem that all our elders are facing. We need more brothers like you, or I fear that we are doomed as a people."

I nodded along with every word that he said. I felt Allah touching my heart with every word that he spoke. I knew what I was supposed to be doing, but the hatred I still had in my heart was stopping me from doing Allah's will. *Just let me kill my enemy, then I'll be all yours.* I felt more than justified to want to kill Lil Juice. His heart was set on killing me for something that I did in my previous lifestyle. I was fully within my rights to keep myself alive and to protect my family from all evil.

"I agree with you, Imam. Just let me pray on it."

Chapter 2
Juice

"Listen to me, blood," Gunna spoke real slow tryna hide his frustration with my stubbornness. He shook his head while he ran his hands through his dreads. "If we go in here, it's a strong possibility that we ain't gon' make it out. And even if we do, we'd have to shoot so many muthafuckaz that they gon' bury us under the jail. Think about this, blood. We ain't welcomed in there." He pointed across the street to the church.

I looked at all the parked cars up and down the street and knew that nobody who drove them had any love for me. They all thought that I killed Naughty and felt nothing but hate and contempt for me. Only Jessie and Naughty's mother, Tammy, knew that I was innocent. Even after I told JoJo about the stunt that Freeze pulled, he still didn't believe me. He claimed that I wanted to put it on Freeze so he would help me kill him on some *Game of Thrones* type of shit!

I stared at the Glock 31 that I gripped in my palm, then made eye contact with my true ride or die nigga. I saw no fear in his eyes, just caution.

"This ain't yo battle, my nigga, sit this one out." I meant it from the heart.

I knew everything that he said was the truth, but I couldn't miss my bitch's funeral. I had to see her one more time. I had to pay my respects to her.

I also needed to see with my own eyes what that bitch ass nigga did to my baby. So whoever had a problem with it was gon' either have to pump the blood out my body or get the fuck out my way!

I bounced out as soon as I read the text from Jessie. *It's time.* I inhaled the cold October air and then stuffed my hands inside the hoody. The bulletproof vest I had on gave me extra confidence that I was gon' walk back out on my own two feet.

Gunna bounced out with a scowl on his face. "If it's our time to die, then we gon' die together. What the fuck I look like sitting in the car while you walk in the lion's den? Let's do this, blood."

I nodded my appreciation then headed across the street. I was done speaking. With each step I climbed up, I felt my anxiety level rise with them. I knew it was a good chance that I would die today. I was literally Portland's Most Wanted! The gas team was out looking for me under the impression that I crushed Jamar. JoJo and all his niggaz were out searching for revenge about Naughty. Those Murk Unit pussies still hadn't got no get back but kept vowing they would. But I didn't give a fuck; I was showing up! And it was just two of us!

I opened the doors and stepped into the pit like the savage I was trained to be. I saw people walking by her coffin, paying their final respects with somber looks on their faces. Jessie was the first person I made eye contact with. She was sitting next to Naughty's mom and Faith.

She waved and gave me a quick smile. Faith turned and saw me, then acted like she saw Satan himself. She gasped then covered her mouth with her hand. *Dramatic bitch.* The tears started really pouring as she stared at me with pure hate in her heart. If she would have been a nigga, I would have had no choice but to put her on my kill list. *I hope she don't make a scene.* I felt multiple people staring at us as we made our way to the casket, but my eyes were locked with her mother's. She found a way to smile at me even though she was experiencing the most pain she'd ever felt. We nodded at each other, and for some reason, I felt a lil better.

The sad music that was being played was really working my emotions. I was doing my best not to let a single tear drop, but it was getting harder and harder. I ignored all the side- eyes as I finally made my way to her body. Pain struck my heart as I stared into her lifeless face. I had to turn and make sure Gunna was seeing what I saw. He shook his head in sadness. I looked back at the woman who I loved the most and regretted every second that I spent away from her. Every argument that we had. "Damn baby, why did you die on me?" I whispered to her.

I stared at her stomach and felt a wave of grief for my unborn child. For all the memories that I would never get to have, I wanted to kill Freeze in the worse way known to man.

When I leaned over and kissed her cold forehead, I finally dropped a tear on her face.

"I'm gon' always love you!" I vowed as I touched my heart.

"No! Let me go! That muthafucka is the one that killed her!" I heard Faith scream from behind me.

Stay calm. I slowly turned around, already knowing that everybody would be staring at me. I put a scowl on my face and poked my chest out for anybody that wanted to challenge my gangsta. I was sick and muthafuckin tired of all the false allegations anyways. Just when I was getting ready to speak up, I locked eyes with Naughty's mother then changed my mind. She shook her head slightly at me, letting me know not to cause a scene. I lasered in on Faith, who was still fronting like she really wanted some smoke with a savage.

I saw JoJo and his niggaz creep out the door, no doubt waiting for me in the hallway. Gunna shrugged his shoulders at what he knew was inevitable. I nodded at my fate, then walked to where I knew my enemies were waiting for me. As soon as we walked into the hallway, ten Drama Gang niggaz were staring at us with hate. The same lil niggaz that used to look at us with admiration were now staring like we were food, and they were a pack of wolves. I'd hate to body somebody or get bodied at her funeral, but there was no way I was going out like a sucka.

"I knew you weren't gon' sneak out the side door," JoJo shook his head as he stepped closer. "Yo pride gon' be the death of you!" He pulled a cannon from his waist.

My eyes never left his as I pulled the Glizzy from my hoody. Wasn't a drop of pussy in my veins, and he knew it firsthand.

"Fuck a side door. Either I'm going out the front, or I'm leaving in a bag, period. But pride ain't got nothing to do with this; it's loyalty. I loved your sister and my unborn. I didn't kill her."

The rest of his niggaz pulled their heat after hearing me deny it. I saw Gunna from my peripheral pull both his guns out.

"On bloods, I'm taking at least four of you niggaz with me. Who ready to die?" He poked his chest out.

"Me!" Ghost shot back and stepped up to the plate.

13

We all pointed our guns at the same time, ready to kill and hoping we didn't get killed in the process. It was a situation that none of us wanted to be in, but it was what it was. I knew I was going to die; we were outgunned by far. My finger was twitching on the trigga, just waiting on the action. I was gon' put a slug right in JoJo's head before I went to meet my maker.

"Put those muthafuckin guns up inside my daughter's funeral! Have y'all lost y'all minds!?" Naughty and JoJo's mom started screaming.

We all looked at her, but none of us lowered our guns. Jessie was standing right next to her, crying and looking scared to death.

"Oh, y'all didn't hear me?" Ms. Patricia walked over and stood right in front of JoJo, blocking his aim at me.

JoJo adjusted his aim at me, and then she blocked it again. I lowered my heat, not wanting to be aiming at the back of her head. I gave Gunna the nod, but he didn't give a fuck. He wasn't dropping his heat until everybody else did.

"Mama, he killed her!" JoJo yelled with tears in his eyes."

"I don't believe he did it. He loves your sister."

"He didn't do it, JoJo. I know he didn't," Jessie defended me too.

"Bitch, fuck you too! If you want, you can die right next to the nigga," he spat at her.

Whap!

Ms. Patricia slapped the shit out of him. He didn't even flinch. He just kept staring through me.

"Watch yo mouth in front of me, nigga, and don't ever disrespect her like that again! Now put that damn gun down!"

He tucked it on his waist then his homies followed suit. Gunna waited until the last gun was gon' before he lowered his.

"I didn't kill her, lil bro. I told you who did it," I tried to convince him again.

"Yeah a'ight, nigga," my words fell on death ears. He put a scowl on his face. "On my sis, you gon' pay for that coffin in there, one way or another, blood," he vowed.

I shook my head at his stupidity, then walked around the group of wolves and made my exit. I made eye contact with all of them. I wanted to see it in their eyes if they thought I really killed her. They did. We walked out into the cold, just happy to be alive and not in handcuffs. Snowflakes were falling from the sky. Winter was officially here, and I didn't expect to be alive or free by the time it was over. Something was telling me to hurry up and kill Freeze, then leave Portland forever. I thought about it was a quick second as I hopped in the whip. Then as fast as it entered my thoughts, I pushed it out. *Fuck that!*

"That's the last time I'm sparing that lil nigga. I don't know about you, but I'm not with all that Mexican standoff shit on bloods. The next time I pull my heat, I'm letting the gunshots speak for me. All this talking and poking my chest out shit is depreciating my gangsta, fo' real," Gunna vowed.

I nodded. "I know, Brody, I just don't wanna kill my lil manz for something I didn't do. I got love for the nigga," I kept it a hunnid.

"Well, he wanna kill you, and that's what it is. We crushin him and his niggaz, simple as that."

Marcellus Allen

Chapter 3
Juice

"Baby! Baby! Get up, look!" my lil sidepiece, Breonna, said as she shook me.

At first, I thought she was waking me up out of one of my nightmares again. I hadn't had one good night of sleep since Naughty and my unborn were killed. Every night she stood over me while I lay in the bed and asked the same question. To make it worse, she had a bullet hole in her face and was holding our dead child in her arms. *"How can you sleep at night knowing that he killed us? Look what he did?"* Then she'd shove the dead child in my face, and I woke up screaming.

"Yo, what's up?" I gripped the Glizzy under the covers.

She pointed at the TV then turned it up. *What the fuck?* What I saw made me shoot straight up while my heart was pounding. They had Flash's face all over the news, wanted for murder and attempted murder. They had a shadow picture next to his with a question mark inside it. As soon as the house niggaz got on the camera, I became all ears.

"He goes by the street name Flash, and we're very familiar with him and his criminal gang. We have all our officials out searching for him as I speak. We will bring him in, and justice will be served. We're still trying to identify the other shooter as well. We have a few leads, but not enough to indict at his time," Detective Freeman said.

She didn't point me out? I couldn't understand for the life of me. I knew she saw my face, especially while I stood over her. I was still amazed that she ate all those bullets and survived it. My phone kept going off, but I wasn't ready to talk. Yet, my mind was racing a million miles a minute. *Gang task lying, I got a warrant too. They're tryna trick me!*

I took a long look at Breonna for any signs of weakness or if the situation was spooking her. I'd been knocking her down on and off since high school, but I had never taken her seriously. Mostly because I was rockin hard body with Latoya, then right after that, I was Britney and Naughty. There wasn't anything wrong with her. She was pretty, light-skinned, had no kids, had a nice body, and did a good job as a nurse. I made my mind up to put her to the test.

"Check this out, baby girl. I need for you to do something important for me."

"Anything you need," she spoke up fast, eager to prove herself.

I nodded. "Okay, look, I need for you to go to my spot and grab all my money out the safe and the guns out the closet too."

"And bring it all here?" she cut me off. From the smile on her face, I knew that's what she wanted.

"Yeah, I'ma need to post over her for like a week or two until I figure some things out. You good with that?"

"Of course, daddy." She leaned over and kissed me. "When do you want me to go?"

I grabbed the keys off of the dresser. "I need you to get on it asap for me before the pigs get the location and get all my shit!"

"Okay. I'm on it." She hopped up and started getting dressed.

I picked up my phone, tired of the muthafucka going off. I told Breonna I'd text her the address, then answered the call. It was Gunna.

"I already know. I'm watching the news right now," I said before he could even get started.

"Pull up at my spot asap."

"Say less."

Chapter 4
Juice

By the time I got to Gunna's spot, everybody was already there waiting for me in the living room. Flash was pacing around the room nonstop, like if he walked faster and faster that maybe our problems would disappear. The stress was evident all over my nigga's face. He was going through it. I looked at TJ, then screwed my face up. I didn't even know his scary ass was back around. I had too many pressing issues to give him too much of my energy, but I did know I wasn't rockin with 'em.

I shook everybody up except for TJ then sat down on the couch. Everybody had on a face of stone wondering what was next for us.

"I told you, nigga. We should have snuck in the hospital and killed that bitch! Now she got the pigs on me!" Flash vented out. He stopped pacing just to stare at me, then started up again.

I felt like he was low key blaming me, but I decided not to check him on it because I knew he was in his feelings and not thinking clearly.

"Don't trip on it. We gon' kill her before she ever takes the stand," I tried to calm his nerves.

He stopped again. "Don't trip? Nigga, I'm wanted for a body plus an attempt. How the fuck I'm not gon' trip? But that's easy for you to say since they ain't looking for you, which I find mighty strange, nigga."

He put it out there, so I had no other choice but to address it. I didn't fully understand what he meant by it, but I was about to get an understanding. I stood up and poked my chest out.

"What you mean you find it strange? What you tryna say, nigga? Huh?" My words were dripping with acid.

"How you not facing an indictment, but I am? You were the one who stood over her, but for some reason, she didn't point you out. It ain't adding up to me."

"You said that to say what? You insinuating that I'm snitchin' or somethin'?" I growled.

I felt my anger getting ready to spill out. If he didn't deny it real fast and, in a hurry, then I was gon' paint the walls and furniture with his blood. Homie or not. I didn't play that snitchin' shit.

He shook his head. "Naw, I ain't saying you a rat, but I am saying somethin' ain't adding up," he clarified.

"Somethin' like what?" Mask asked.

I took a quick glance at Gunna, and he shook his head, letting me know not to do it. When I looked at TJ, he had a lil smirk on his face that he was tryna hide. It took everything in me not to shoot it off his face.

"Like somebody behind the scenes only want me to go to jail. Maybe those Murk Unit niggaz had her snitch on me, but not Juice, so they could kill him. She probably told them one of us had to go to jail, and they chose me."

"It's possible," Mask replied.

"Or she just can't really remember what bro looks like. Witnesses get it wrong all the time," Gunna spoke up.

"I think they are lying on the gang. They probably just tryna catch me lackin' while they're building more cases on me." I sat back down and exhaled while I ran my fingers through my dreads. "Ain't no way she ain't snitch on me."

The room got quiet while everybody was deep in their own thoughts. Something wasn't right, and we all knew it.

"So what you gon' do, turn yourself in?" TJ broke the silence.

Flash gave him a crazy nigga look. "Nigga, what? They gon' have to come get me, and that's on Omar's grave. You feel me, nigga?" He and Gunna shook up with faces full of arrogance. Hearing the words 'Omar's grave' gave me the chills and made me feel like murdering something. I knew I wouldn't be able to sleep until I put everybody that was involved inside a casket, a closed one. Freeze killed Jamar, but Pusha and Flip were gonna die by the bullets I pumped into their bodies. I looked over at TJ. *I should kill him right now.* My hand eased closer to my waist while I bit down on my lip. I didn't know why, but my spirit kept telling me not to trust the nigga. I knew he didn't set Omar up 'cause if he did, the streets would have been talking. No matter how hard niggaz tried to keep the covers over slimy backdoor situations, it always gets leaked. My true problem was that he left bro to die in the street by himself. Omar would have never left him like that. Never.

"And we lost the connect too? So, what we gon' do now?" TJ stared through me. I felt the accusations through his eyes.

"I don't care what you do, nigga," I spat.

"Y'all don't start that shit," Mask jumped in before it got outta hand.

"I say we run off on the plug, get those last bricks he promised us, then tell 'em to come get it in blood. My lil niggaz need some work, and we damn near out. We don't owe that nigga no loyalty no more. He just cut us off for no reason right when we need him the most," Gunna laid out his plan.

Rob O-Dawg? It didn't sit right with me for some reason. He was the only nigga that I ever considered my big homie. The only man that ever put food on my plate. But he did take away the whole plate just because he felt that we were too hot.

"Nah, I ain't feelin' that one, rob O-Dawg? That's one that we'll end up regretting. He gon' put a bag on all of our heads and all the so-called wolves gon' try to collect," I replied.

"And? Name a time when somebody wasn't tryna kill us? The only difference is we'll have the money and the dope to fight back with. Oh, and on bloods, that pussy nigga Twin definitely been out here selling the same work as us."

I nodded along, already knowing the truth. That one really got under my skin more than anything else.

"If we rob O-Dawg, then we gotta kill everybody that's connected with him," Mask spoke the truth.

"That's coo with me," Flash shrugged his shoulders. "I don't like Twin or that bougie nigga Jaxx anyways. How I'm feeling right now, anybody can get it, and that's on the set."

I thought deeply about what they were saying, weighing the pros and cons. It would be a dangerous move that could cost us our lives if we didn't do it right. I felt my loyalty towards O start evaporating more and more with each thought.

"Y'all sure y'all wanna do this? We gon really be Portland's most wanted fo'real."

Everybody nodded their heads with no hesitation, sealing our fates. We were in too deep, and only a casket could take us out of the streets. Our list of enemies was too long to count, and we added to it on the daily. But at the top of mine was Freeze, and I refused to die or go to jail before I drained every drop of blood out of his soft ass body.

Chapter 5
Juice

A few nights later and it was back on. We had heard from a couple of loyal hoodrats that Dirty and Teflon were out clubbing with their Murk Unit niggaz like they ain't have a care in the world. These folks were out poppin' bottles like they didn't know that some real wolves wanted to pop their tops. But it was coo' with us cause while they were busy wanting to be seen, we were on the way to see them.

I was riding shotgun with Gunna while Mask, TJ, and Flash followed in the whip behind us.

"I can't wait to crush that nigga Dirty, he out here moving like he bulletproof or something! Like there ain't no consequences for snatching my chain, this nigga must be crazy." I vented to Gunna while I grabbed both .40's that were lying on my lap.

"Believe that. But why the hell can't we get a line on this nigga Freeze? It's like he's disappeared into thin air. Ain't nobody seen 'em, heard from 'em, or nothing. I wanna kill him so bad that I can't even sleep at night. It's all I think about. That nigga killed my brotha in front of me and my moms, and now he has his chain. You know how that makes me look? How that makes me feel?"

He parked, then stared into my eyes. One lost soul to another, demon to demon.

"Yeah, I know 'cause I feel the same way, nigga. He was my big bro too. That's why we bout to start our killin spree right now."

I nodded and then stepped into the chilly November night. Mask, TJ, and Flash got out of their car and met us at the trunk. We all had guns out, and our eyes locked across the street at the club parking lot. It was definitely poppin' out there and would only get more crowded as the club closed. My blood started boiling just knowing that my enemies were somewhere close.

"How y'all wanna do it? Y'all wanna walk up or what?" Flash spoke up.

"It's too crowded for that shit. We'll get spotted before we can scope them out. Plus, I ain't tryna have to run back across this busy street," I responded.

"Why don't y'all park in the lot, and we'll park on the side of the building? That way, we'll pin them in on both sides," TJ suggested.

Even though I couldn't stand the sound of his voice, I couldn't deny that his plan made the most sense. I looked at Gunna, and he nodded his approval.

"Y'all wait 'til we start bustin' before y'all up it. I'm gonna wait 'til I see Dirty before I bounce out, then it's on. We gon' send 'em running towards y'all, and then y'all knock 'em down, on gang," I said, then turned away.

I put on my ski mask soon as I got back inside and switched to killah mode. I couldn't wait to hop back out and let them .40's do their thang.

I leaned the seat back as soon as Gunna pulled into the lot. My heart started racing as I tried to discreetly scan the lot for any sign of Dirty. The club was just closing, so it was niggaz and women everywhere tryna be seen or tryna be chosen. I recognized a few faces, but nothing too serious. Gunna parked real discreetly, then we really started studying everybody in sight. I spotted a few suckaz I didn't really feel because they hung out with the opps, but I didn't feel like wasting any shells on some nobodies.

"There go Teflon right there on the set," he growled.

"Nigga where?" I turned towards him.

"Right there." He pointed to a group of niggaz that was posted on a Benz while they spitted game to a group of females.

They were so comfortable that they weren't even watching their surroundings or nothing. That had me hotter than anything.

"These niggaz think we really pussy, huh?" I questioned.

Gunna didn't respond, but I saw his face get screwed up. I knew that meant he saw something that had him hot. I followed his eyes and saw exactly the sucka that I came looking for. *Dirty and Shotta!* It was just the two of them walking.

I slid out with my twin demons on demon time, ready to send them bitch nigga to party with Mac Dre.

Bloaw! Boca! Boca! Bloaw! Boca!

Shots started smackin' from all over, forcing us to hide between parked cars.

"Blood, we got set up, gang," Gunna growled, crouched down across from me.

I bit chap off my bottom lip while my blood boiled with anger, and a couple more names were added to my death list.

"Don't trip, gang. We gon' drop every nigga involved, starting with these pussies," I swore, then let the vengeful demon in me navigate my moves.

"Niggas don't want it with the Drama," a very familiar voice taunted while throwing shots.

I ran a lil plan across Gunna, and then we put the play in motion.

I crept low, moving in between parked cars until I caught the side of a shoe. I knew none of my niggas would be caught dead wearing. Since whoever the shoe had belonged to had been on the other end of the parking lot, I couldn't just jump to my feet and let the fire spark. I followed the Team Jordan through the lot and got upset after finding a nigga dead that I needed to kill in order to calm the savage beast in me.

"Cuz...help me," Dirty begged with a hole in his chest lying next to some half-decent-looking bitch covered in blood.

My adrenaline shot through the ceiling after hearing his bitch ass cry for help. I stood up, no longer fearing death, and looked at the pussy. "Cry to them bitch niggas who left you to die."

Boca, Boca!!

I dropped two in his face silencing his cries, and continued scratching names off my opps list.

The Devil always favors the Demon, I thought after seeing Teflon trying to run back in the club.

Boca, Boca!!

Teflon knocked down a civilian after receiving a back shot.

"Swish! Chef Curry with the shot, boy," Gunna celebrated.

"I'd been so focused on getting I didn't even hear Gunna creep up on me. Just as I started to cut through the crowd to finish Teflon off, somebody shoved me to the ground.

Bloaw! Bloaw! Boca! Boca!

I looked up and saw the unexpected. TJ had been blowing for me. He was really moving the crowd, not caring who he'd hit all for the love of the gang.

"Come on. We gotta go." Gunna helped me up while TJ kept pushing forward, tryin' a kill whoever tried knocking me off.

People were running wild, scrambling for their lives, but throughout all the gunplay, they still found time to hold out their phones in hopes of capturing the moment.

The sound of cop sirens forced us to abort the mission and escape with our freedom.

Chapter 6
Freeze

"Cuz, we really got shit crackin' with these pills. I'm seeing more money than I have ever seen," the homie, Nutcase, said.

I didn't wanna believe that pain killers would bring in more and faster money than coke, but Trey's vision had become clear the moment he dropped fifty racks on my wife. And after coming home, he dropped over a hunnid up. All praises went to Allah for me being able to provide for my family while being in jail.

"On the dead Locs, I didn't think it would be like this, cuz," I confessed, holding a stack of blues I haven't counted yet.

We were posted at Trey's side piece's spot in Beaverton. We weren't trying to handle business around females, but after Trey told me he'd sent the bitch out shopping, I made my cameo. Plus, being with Trey got Fatima off my back. With Trey being a devoted Muslim to the public, Fatima encouraged me to be around him more.

"Yea cuz the paper fo'sho straight, but there's a real killa on the loose gunnin' for you. We gotta get him out the way fast." Forty kicked fads.

"We can fall back and let the streets take him out. He either die like his brotha or in a cell like his idol," Cash said.

Even though Cash spoke the ghetto gospel, it would be much more satisfying knowing his momma had to bury both of her sons because of me. Thinking back on how I did bitchass Big Juice brought a smile across my face. *He shouldn't have put his hands on a real nigga.*

"Fuck waiting for Karma to strike. Let's bring it to the slob now." Problem dapped Nutcase.

"Naw loco. We gon' catch that nigga when he least expects it. On Top-Gun," hearing Trey say my dead cousin's name low key struck a nerve. I spent many days hittin' laps on that prison yard after seeing Top-Gun's face on the news.

Young black male shot dead during an attempted car jackin'.

It felt like my Crippin' had gotten slapped across the face.

An hour and some change after our meeting, I had to hit the Mosque with my queen and princess to bring more structure to my life. Killing that pregnant lady didn't fuck with me nearly as much as smoking an innocent Crip, but that's something I would have to handle with Tookie when I make it to the other side.

"Lonzo, the change you've made to be a better husband, a great father, and an all-around better man brings peace to my life. I only dreamed of living," Fatimah gave me credit from the passenger seat.

I stared into her beautiful brown eyes and smiled. "Allah Akhbar." I looked in the backseat and found Aaliyah knocked out cold.

The Imam had been outside the Mosque talking to a young Muslim brother. My eyes met with the Imams, causing him to flash a smile as I helped my family out of the car and greeted my brothers.

Chapter 7
Juice

I thought losing Naughty, and our unborn child would be the hardest thing I'd gone through in my adult life after losing Omar, but nothing hurt more than finding out a nigga that I'd been willing to put it all on the line for tried lining me. And to make matters worse, he didn't even come for me himself. He put some no-name niggas on me, but for some reason, my love for him hadn't dropped a bit. I still wanted him to come to his senses and realize I didn't kill his sister.

"Pappi, I know this is hard for you to believe, but nothing's gonna stop him from coming at you."

I just stared at the pile of powda in front of me, knowing Jessie's words had been exactly what I needed to hear, but I'd been leaning towards what I wanted to hear.

"No matter what I said, I could never bring myself to take Naughty's life." Painful tears fell from my eyes. "Even after everything, I still wanted to build a family with her." I scooped a nice coke mountain with my I.D. and took whatever didn't fall to the nostril.

Jessie scooted closer to me and wiped my face dry. "Look at you. You're such a mess, Pappi." She ran her hands through my dreads and started massaging my scalp. "You know what you gotta do, Davointae."

All I heard was Naughty's voice saying my government, so my head had relaxed against what I believed to be Naughty's breast.

"Baby, you don't understand."

"I might be the only person who does, Pappi."

Before I'd been able to pull away after realizing I hadn't been in Naughty's arms, Jessie had taken full advantage of my vulnerability.

She'd begin loosening my belt while sucking on my neck.

I couldn't name one real nigga who fought off a bad bitch they haven't fucked yet. I didn't have ties to any bitch, so I lifted my arms up and let her lift my shirt over my head. She tossed it, then ran her tongue down my chest, snatched my jeans down, and started sucking me.

Thew!

She spit something nasty on my semi-hard dick, sucked it off, then looked up at me with spit drippin down the side of her mouth. "It tastes better than I thought."

My hand hit the back of her head, sending her back to work. Even with all the coke in my system, she'd gotten me rock hard in minutes.

"Come get it, Pappi Juice," she purred, pulling her sweats down as she stood up with her fat ass bouncing in my face while she grabbed her ankles.

"So, this what you want, huh?" I smacked her ass, making her purr.

She sucked some air in and then confessed what I already knew. "I've been wanting to feel you inside of me since I saw you. Oh, shit, Pappi. I feel it in places nobody has ever been... Ahh! Shit! Fuck! Pull my hair."

I ignored her demands and tried pounding my stress away with every pump, then reality struck after I came.

Never had I ever felt guilty about who I fucked, but after smashin' Jessie, something just didn't sit right with me. I fought my guilt with the fact Jessie was the one who tried saving my life by warning me about JoJo trying to backdoor me, but I didn't check my phone until after the club shooting. I'd seen too many crime shows where niggas had gotten convicted because their phones pinged off on a tower near the incident at the same time the incident had gotten reported. For that reason, I kept my phone at the crib whenever I went on a drill. I refused to get sentenced to die in jail by the hands of technology. A witness would have to survive some shots, then point me out in court.

"Was that everything?" Breonna asked, breaking my train of thought.

"Yea, that was everything, baby," I confirmed from the edge of the bed, watching the news for any updates on the Kim situation.

It didn't surprise me to hear how hard the house niggas had been pressing the streets for answers. What did surprise me was that my name still hadn't come up in any of it.

I stared at the duffel bag that sat next to me filled with money I probably would never live long enough to spend. What I would be able to do is make sure my lil girls were taken care of, but the only issue with that's getting it to them. Baby momma number one had gotten content with a soft nigga, and baby momma number two just wasn't fuckin' with me. Shit in the streets been so hot, I hadn't physically spent time with my lil girls in a minute, but that didn't stop me from jumpin' on Facetime with them daily.

"Daddy, you seem stressed." Breonna started massaging my shoulders from behind me.

She hit it right on the nose. My mind had been in so many places that stress had been the best way to sum my mood up with one word.

"Naw, I'm Gucci, baby," I capped behind a fake smile.

Ring, ring, ring...

"Let me get that for you." She snatched my phone off the dresser. "It's Gunna"

"What up, gang?"

"Guess who baby momma I ran into?"

I damn near tripped over my shoelace, rushing out the house to meet Gunna.

Marcellus Allen

Chapter 8
Freeze

Between religion and family, I barely had time to find bitch ass Lil Juice. I wasn't for all the social media internet shit these new era niggas done became obsessed with. I had too much going on in my life to bring down the value of my Crip by putting my business out there for the world to see, but Allah works in ways a man could never predict.

"Cuz, we gon' bring this Rose City Crip shit all the way back with this one," Nutcase boasted from the driver seat of a Caravan.

I had love for the homie and respected his get down when it came to bringing back the gang, but I never liked the fact he spoke real loose in front of new niggas, and that's just who the nigga in the passenger seat was to me, a new nigga.

"We gon' be known for real after this one loco. This one gotta bring the bitch nigga to his knees."

I just stared at the nappy-headed nigga disgusted at hearing his nasty deep voice.

We were posted a block away from the Vill waiting to go up two bodies and make that bitch ass slob lil Juice feel the same pain I felt when his bitch ass took Top Gun from me.

"Cuz who the fuck are you anyway?" I got tired of hearing the lil nigga run his mouth.

"Lil nuts. I'm Nutcase's lil bro, the one who dropped that rack on yo books cuz." He explained like I should show some love to a nigga I didn't give a fuck about.

I scooted to the edge of the seat so they could hear me loud and clear. "First off, I don't know you for you to be talkin' all carefree around me," I faced Nutcase, already feelin' him stare at me, so I let that nigga know what type of time I'm on. "Cuz, you know I don't do all the new niggas. Keep yo friends and lil homies far from me." I leaned back in my seat and relaxed. "Cuz, you givin' Crip'n a black eye with this one."

"I don't know who you think you checkin' homie, but we been out here pushin' since you been gone," Nutcase turned, faced me, and tried holding his own. "We respect you as being one of the OG's who started the RCC shit, all that high power disrespectful shit, nigga, I ain't fo'. And Top Gun is the one who loc'd cuz in. He just got my name 'cause he's my lil brotha."

"I said what I said, cuz. But if Top Gun C.I.P liked him enough to put him on, then that's enough for me."

Nutcase pulled a flip phone from his pocket. "Them niggas are coming out right now."

We jumped out in the light snow, hoodied down and masked up. We got about twenty feet from a black-on-black G-Wagon that looked pretty parked over a small snow pile.

Nutcase tapped Lil Nuts and signaled from him to creep across the street while we stepped forward, using parked cars to shield us.

"Together, we can run this dope shit from the A to Portland, blood. You get ungrateful ass, Ju-"

"Rose City Crip!" Lil Nuts banged the set and got it crackin'.

Boca! Boca! Boca! Boca!

Shots rang out from both sides, waking the block up.

Nutcase stepped in the middle of the street, letting off as if death didn't fade him.

I got low and crept until I felt I'd been close enough to score.

"Tell Juice his brotha gon' be up there soon," I growled while bussin' tryin' a knock Twin head off.

I had to give it to Lil Nuts he ran down on them niggas clackin'. He was on their heels. He had them niggas backing up, throwing shots at anything behind them while running like the bitch niggas they are.

Boca! Boca! Boca! Boca! Boca! Boca!

Car doors, apartment buildings, trees, and windows all received shells.

Yea, it is over for cuz.

JoJo fell face first in a pile of snow and dropped his smack.

Boca Boca Boca Boca!!!

Twin got Ricky'd with a back shot, flying against the gate. He slid down and didn't move a muscle.

I started speed walking towards the JoJo nigga while trying not to slip on the icy ground.

"Fuck crabs, Drama Gang," a nigga who couldn't be no older than seventeen yelled while running out the building and swingin' a Draco.

I tried getting out of there so fast, I crashed on the ice and dropped my smack.

"Fuck!" I spat, landing on my shoulder.

"I'm hit, cuz."

I looked to the left of me and saw Nutcase on the ground about ten feet from me, lying next to his strap and bleeding.

"Cuz, we gotta catch these niggas another time." I scooped up my gun, crouched down, and made my way to the homie.

"Cuz, get up! We gotta go! One time on the way." I kneeled over him, looking at the hole in his chest and shoulder, waiting for him to respond.

His hand covered the hole in his chest, and then he let out a couple of coughs. "Cuz get my hat and tell Lil Nuts, we out."

The shots stopped, and the sirens got loud. I wrapped one of Nutcase's skinny arms over my shoulder and moved as fast as I could to the van.

"Where Lil Nuts?"

The look on his face after receiving the news that his lil bro didn't make it had to be the same face I wore when I found out about Top Gun.

I laid the homie down in the backseat and consoled him while hopping in the driver's seat. "He went out like a G. He took Twin with him." As I pulled off, I saw Lil Nuts trying to pick himself up with three holes in his chest. His eyes lit up with hope when he saw me, but I turned my head fast, giving the road all my attention while hittin' the gas even faster.

Marcellus Allen

Chapter 9
Juice

"You think he in there?" I asked, sitting in the passenger seat of his black Impala.

"Blood, she all over the nigga's I.G. and Facebook page on some family time with a lil boy that looks dead on his ugly ass, on the Gang," Gunna replied while pulling a half-smoked blunt from the ashtray.

We were parked in West Salem across the street from the spot Trey and his family shared.

I couldn't pinpoint it, but something just didn't feel right about the situation. I knew Trey to be Freeze's day one, but I couldn't remember a time where I'd seen any Rose City Crips doing any social media beefin' or posting about anything. Shit got to the point where I thought they were extinct. None of us had phones on us just in case we had to body somebody.

I should have seen how recent them pictures were.

"Gang, we can't be out here sitting on these nice ass clean streets all day and expect for someone not to call the Boys." I got the blunt and took a long pull, feelin' the stress that came with the current situation slowly drop while I held the smoke in my chest, then slowly exhaled.

"We ain't blockin' no driveways. Plus, with all this rain coming down, ain't nobody looking out the windows. You ain't got no warrants, and you ain't on papers, blood." He got the blunt, hit it, then continued his lil rant, "It ain't like we be out here anyway. All we gotta do is make it."

"I don't need you to coach me through shit." I put a stop to all that bullshit. He felt the need to speak out loud.

"I ain't gon' knock you, blood." He hit the weed and leaned in towards me. "I'll take you home if this shit is startin' to fuck with you…" He hit the doobie, then handed it to me.

I knew bro was just tryin' to be funny, but I had too much going to make time for all his fuckery. Here his ass tryin' to joke and shit.

We sat in the car for hours, smoking blunt after blunt and pissing in soda bottles while waiting for a grey 2015 Honda truck.

"We've been out here for damn near half the day."

"There it goes right there." Gunna pointed out, being hella extra like always.

I pulled my beanie down and zeroed in, following the truck anxiously with my eyes ready to strike.

It seemed like the rain started shooting from the sky as we slid our moving scandalous trying to beat the garage door from closing.

The bitch had been pulling groceries bags out the back seat with her phone in her hand, sounding hella ratchet.

"I'm a take TJ to my momma's house, and we out there tonight, girl. So tell that nigga he better take a Molly because I'm a put it on that nigga bitch!"

The bitch had been so locked in on her phone call she didn't even notice us slide through the garage just as the door closed.

She'd been about ten to fifteen pounds over my weight limit for a bitch, but she did have fat ass for a white girl. I couldn't get a look at her face because she'd been walking in the house still running her mouth.

I could feel Gunna growing irritated with the process, but we didn't know who else had been in the house, and I couldn't afford no nosey neighbors calling the Po-Po saying they heard shots. Judging by the neighborhood we were in, the cops would be through in seconds.

"Bitch, I gotta put these groceries up. I'm a call you back." She tried closing the door with her foot, but Gunna stopped the door with his foot.

Smack!

"Ah shit!" she yelled from the left hook Gunna gave her, causing all types of snacks to go flying in the air as her phone flew to the living room.

I just knew she was out cold after seeing how hard she landed on that tile floor. She stood on all fours, shook that shit off, and rose to her feet with a light wobble.

"She wants smoke, gang." I couldn't believe what had just happened.

I'd never seen a nigga dope fiend a bitch and not knock her out. The shit had been pure comedy, but I had to save the laughs for a later date. There was too much on the line.

"Bitch, if you don't quit it." I upped on her. "We want yo weak ass baby daddy."

She made a screw face. "I ain't no snitch. You got me fucked up, nigga!"

Whap!

"Bitch, I shoulda smoked you the first time you said nigga. You ain't black, blood." Gunna barked after hitting her with the ass of his gun and finally knocking her out.

"Find something to tie the bitch up. I'm a check the house make sho' ain't nobody here."

"If somebody was here, they would have been coming after I dropped that bitch the first time."

I knew Gunna not knocking the bitch out the first time he punched her low-key fucked with his pride, but I needed bro to get his head the game. The mission hadn't even started, and it seemed like we weren't seeing eye to eye.

"Momma."

My head shot to the direction the voice came from and got greeted by a lil mixed boy who looked no older than three.

I don't know if my stomach could take killing another child.

"Are you guys some more uncles I never met yet?" the lil boy asked.

Gunna and I looked at each other and shrugged, not knowing how to answer.

"I know who you are? Uncle Deion and Uncle Jeff. Y'all tried to trick me. Now you can take the mask off." The boy named us, giving me an idea for the perfect plan.

Chapter 10
Freeze

I had just hopped out of the shower after washing off all the blood from the homie off me. I dropped Nutcase off at the hospital and prayed Allah saved him, but Lil Nuts was already gone in my eyes. The way them lil slob niggas were getting' off, I'll be surprised if cuz made it out paralyzed.

My phone started lighting as I'd been drying off.

"What's crackin'?" I answered in a low tone, so I didn't wake up Fatimah.

"Cuz gone..." Forty cried the news to me.

I sat the toilet seat down and let out a long sigh. "I don't' even know what to say? But Cuz went out dumpin' on the set fo' real. Both of em."

"Cuz, on Top Gun..." tears of pain had been all in his voice.

Honestly, I felt him because I had love for Nutcase, but I had a mission, and that's to kill that bitch nigga, Lil Juice before he killed me. I couldn't believe how hard it's been trying to find somebody who loved being seen.

"Don't even trip. We gon' get em for Nutcase and Lil Nuts," I vowed.

"Naw fam. Nutcase didn't make it, but Lil Nuts is in the I.C.U. room."

I parked my face in my palm, not knowing exactly how to move. I just knew Lil Nuts wouldn't make it, but after hearing Cuz had been in the I.C.U. Him not making it's the only thing I can hope for.

Forty wanted to ride on them marks, but I had to convince him how hot shit had gotten, and we didn't have a direct line on any of them clowns and all that riding around looking for people's something I'm not playing a participant in. They better find some young niggas for that.

I turned my phone off and took a peek into my daughter's room. Watching her sleep freely without a care in the world made me think of the innocent child's life I took before it even started.

Allah, please forgive me.

I quietly closed her door and went to me and Fatimah's room. Just staring at her made me wanna change my life. She helped me walk down a decade, and the only thing she wanted was for me to put my family first.

"You just got back, King?" Fatimah asked, half-sleep as I slid in the bed with her.

"I just took the trash out," I lied as I wrapped her in my arms.

"You smell fresh," she fished, lightly interrogating me, and hoping to catch me slippin'.

"I ain't gon hop in the bed with my queen all filthy." I kissed her on the cheek.

"Bet not?" She backed that fat ass up against my dick, and shit got real.

Chapter 11
Juice

We tied the bitch up, gagged her mouth, and strapped her to the chair. Gunna wanted to do the same to the lil nigga and just tell him it's part of a game we were playing, but I couldn't do another child, so Gunna just took the lil nigga in his room and played x-box with him.

"We gon' see how much yo bitch ass baby daddy loves you and yo ugly ass son," I taunted, holding her phone.

Her eyes got wide as she fought to get loose while trying to yell, but it had been close to impossible for someone to be heard with a gag tied across their mouth and duct tape covering their lips.

I slow scrolled down to bitch ass Trey's name just to antagonize her thot ass.

"What's crackin, cuz?" he answered, sounding all hard and shit with a group of niggas on borrowed time in the background.

There wasn't shit for me to say. I just put the phone on the bitch.

"What is this a joke, cuz?" He had his friends in the back laughing doing ad-libs.

"Naw, this real-life, bitch nigga. Now, these are yo choices. You can give me bitch ass Alphonzo's address, or you can give life for the life of yo bitch and son"

"Cuz, I ain't giving my nigga up or giving my life for that bitch and her baby. Do me a favor. I'm tired of paying child support."

The line went dead, leaving me with only one option.

I walked to a bedroom which seemed long as fuck as I tried blocking out my conscious.

I opened the door to find Gunna playing X-Box with his mask off, and the lil nigga had been knocked out sleep in his lil bed.

When Gunna came into the hallway, I told him how the phone call went down.

"Fuck that blood. Call his bitch ass back, and I'm a show 'em what he did to his son!"

Those who knew me would say I'd gone soft, but I couldn't have a hand in killing a lil kid.

"We ain't gotta do shit to the lil nigga. Just lock 'em in the room, blood."

I looked Gunna in his eyes. "You going soft on me, gang?"

"Never that, gang. It's he ain't see us, and the crab nigga said you take 'em off child support, right?"

I nodded.

"If he outlives us, his son gon' kill him for him being the reason his momma's dead, and the nigga still got fifteen years of paying child support." He let out a lil laugh.

We put knives in the door's ledge, locking the lil nigga in, then we got the show started.

"Cuz, why you playing on my phone?"

"Call his bluff, cuz," somebody who'd been with him made a deadly suggestion.

The only nigga I recognized had been Problem, but I didn't see the bitch nigga, Freeze, anywhere. Just looking at them bitch niggas got me hot. Not one of them hoe niggas on that screen fired a gun in over a decade.

"What I do, fam? Those were Top Gun's last words," I taunted with a smirk.

I woke the whole crowd up with that one. I got called slob in so many different ways, it cracked up Gunna. I never thought I would live to see the day Gunna would hear the word 'slob' and not trip, but the death threats from niggas we knew didn't wanna kill nothing or let nothing a crack up and real killa.

"On Rose City Crip, I'm a kill you, nigga." Trey pulled his gansta from wherever it had been.

I looked at Gunna while I held the screen at the bitch's face.

Her eyes kept blinking while she tried wiggling out the situation. Tears flew down her face messing up her make-up, and that's when I knew it finally hit her that she'd been seconds from meeting her maker all because she chose to have a baby with a bitch nigga.

I gave Gunna the go.

Boca! Boca! Boca!!!

"Oh, shit! Cuz is crazy," one of them bitch niggas said after Gunna dropped two in her face.

Splashes of blood slapped the screen and rushed to the floor. I didn't even wipe the screen off. I wanted to really fuck with him for talking that high-power shit.

"Look what you did bring the bitch nigga you are." I let out a sinister and hung up on him.

"If a nigga don't slide 'bout that, he gotta be snitch," Gunna said, then tapped me on the chest. "Let's blow this joint."

"Hol' up."

I cleaned the screen off, took pictures of the dead bitch, sent them to every contact in the phone. Afterwards, I tossed the phone on the dead bitch, and we got outta' there.

Marcellus Allen

Chapter 12
Freeze

"Cuz, this shit ain't right," Trey stressed, running a hand down his face.

We were at Cash's spot in Vancouver, catching up on the triv in his basement. The homies were passing blunts and sippin' syrup.

I don't knock niggas for how they live because I'd once been misled before joining the Nation, but after sitting in jail watching people pop pill after pill to get through their sentence and doing drugs unheard of to real niggas I chose to cleanse myself of anything that can slow me down.

"Cuz, you tried calling that lil nigga's bluff," Problem brought new evidence to the table.

"That don't even sound right, bro. You gon' play with yo son and his mom, cuz?" I looked at Trey with nothing but pure disappointment.

I couldn't believe a man of his caliber would even play like that with a nigga who's killing for his pride.

"Cuz, this ain't a time to be playing." Trey stood up with both fists balled with a look in his eyes I hadn't seen in over a decade.

Problem stood up and met the challenge with that down for whatever look on his face.

None of the others tried breaking them from their pre-boxing match stare down, and that's when I knew shit had been cooking for a while.

Forty stepped in between them and mediated, "You niggas wanna wait 'til we down a homie to start trippin. We got a pack of wolves after us now in real-time. Fuck how we got here. How we gon' get outta this?"

I noticed two of three lil homies who were in attendance started picking sides, favoring Problem.

"Shit, all we gotta do is give back the chain."

My head slowly swung towards Cash's direction. I stood up, stepped in his face, and put him in his place.

"Cuz, you sound like a bitch," my index finger banged his chest while I continued checkin' him. "Get yo ass beat in yo house playin' with my crip'n." I pulled my Dickie's over my waist and looked up at him with a cold killa's mug. "What you wanna do, cuz? I've been itching to max a nigga out."

His six-foot five-inch lanky frame towered over my five-foot eight-inch bulky body, but I knew his hand game couldn't fuck with mine.

He stood strong, looking tough, trying to save face for the crowd, but real killas smelled fear like Vampires do blood.

"Juice got smoked because the foot of every Hit-Squad nigga touched yo face. I smoked the slob in front of his momma to show niggas my crip'n is real. You couldn't stomach the shit." I looked at the young locs. "Cuz threw up after the body dropped."

Everybody started rollin' printing and laughing at mark-ass Cash.

"No wonder Cuz never go on drills with us. Always talkin' 'bout niggas gotta get their hood credibility up before he slides with 'em," Lazy instigated exposing Cash in his own house in front of every nigga that mattered to the gang.

Putting homies on blast who had rank in front of the lil homies had never been my style but hearing weak-nigga shit had brought the person out of me I tried hard on leaving behind me in that cell I'd left.

"Look, homie," Trey's deep, commanding voice had gotten everyone's attention.

"Cuz, we ain't 'posed to be getting at each other like this. We all Rose City Crips. One problem is all of our problems. And right now, the root of our problem is Lil Juice." Trey had every one of us dappin' each other and apologizing to each other.

Truthfully, Trey had been the only person in the room I planned on fucking with after we killed Lil Juice. I learned from the situation with Nutcase and Lil Nuts that embracing the young locs only made you more of a harder target to hit because your enemies would have to get through them to get to you.

Linking up with the young locs had been my main reason for coming to Cash's spot and to check on the homie, Trey.

"Cuz, what happened with Kaylah and yo lil man?" I asked.

A look of guilt mixed with depression covered his face as he pulled his phone out and scrolled down to what he wanted me to see, and then handed me the phone.

"Look for yo' self, and the homie is right. I did it," he finally confessed.

These pictures were gruesome. They blew holes through the innocent woman right in her living room. It looked nasty. I knew we had to turn up the heat that very minute, and I knew just how to get Lil Juice's attention.

Marcellus Allen

Chapter 13
Juice

I sat on Gunna's couch, trying to sip my pain away with six ounces of Lean in a liter of Sprite, but I couldn't stop thinking about Naughty.

You 'posed to here with me.

Shit had gotten so crazy I even caught myself calling Breonna, Naughty a few times, and Breonna had me I'd been having conversations with Naughty in my sleep.

Breonna's so much of a good bitch that she didn't even trip off the shit. She just wanted to be there for me while I'd been drowning in pain, so I decided to give her some space and tap in with the gang.

Everybody had been in attendance kickin' the triv just really catching up, but me. I'd been in my own world deep in thought until some good news hit the air.

"Yea, gang, the nigga Twin is in the hospital right now. Them niggas got in a clack-out and he must ain't have his smack on him 'cause he got hit in the back," Mask explained, standing up twistin' a wood.

"Aye, when that shit happened?" I sat my cup down and pulled out my phone, checkin' social media for the triv.

"Just the other day," Flash answered from the couch that he, TJ, and Gunna sat on.

"I don't know how a nigga missed that? The bitch nigga Nutcase finally came out from hibernating after being on a fifteen-year hiatus and got smoked, and then they put his lil homie in the I.C.U. room." Mask lit the blunt.

I'd been so out of touch with shit going on in the streets because I had to lay low after smoking that innocent lady. But to hear Twin took a back shot had made me smile.

Nutcase getting smoked only meant them Rose City Crips were out to get me and anyone they felt had been a part of my team.

I looked at Gunna, and he shrugged his shoulders, letting me know he'd also been left in the dark about the shit.

"They say the lil nigga Ghost saved them niggas and dropped at least thirty out the Draco," TJ said chillin' on the couch, the only nigga in the room sober.

"You know that mean blood?" Gunna asked, then scooted to the edge of the couch," That mean that hoe ass nigga Freeze got them hoe niggas slidin' really tryin' a crush bro and any nigga with him."

TJ waved it off with a hand jester. "Them niggas ain't nobody to worry about. They caught Twin and JoJo slippin coming out the Vill."

Hearing JoJo damn near getting shot fucked with me for real. I really looked at him like he was my lil brotha. Even after the shot-out at the club, I still wanted him to believe and know I didn't kill his sister but being a real stubborn my way or no way type of person, I knew firsthand that it took more than words to convince him.

"Blood, I don't know what you heard, but sleepin' on an opp ain't ever been how Gang rock." Gunna took a sip of his double cup then started fucking with his phone.

"If we gon' get 'em, we need to get a line on 'em first," TJ finally said something that made sense and would benefit the gang.

I took half of a Perc 30, washed down with some Lean, then I hit the weed. I sat back and thought about my next play for some money.

Since we had half the city on us really trying to bring it to us, it seemed like the money had slowed up a lot.

And that fuck nigga, Twin, sellin the same work at a lower price.

Just the thought of a nigga taking food out of my babies' mouths really fucked with me, and the plug scared of a lil heat.

"Y'all still got work?" I needed to know because a person's hunger would determine how far they're willing to go.

"I'm down to the bottom blood, so we need to set that play to lash the plug in motion." Gunna's face didn't leave his screen.

Every one of my niggas was either down to the last or almost there. The missing piece of the puzzle to robbing your plug is who do you cop from next.

"We need to figure out how we gon' get that bougie nigga, Jaxx. 'Cause after we do that, we gon' have a new level of beef," Flash pointed out, getting the blunt from Mask.

"This bitch ass nigga, blood." Gunna sprang to his feet, low-key working my nerves with his lil extra antics and shit. He pointed at the screen as if the person could see him, "Bitch nigga I'm a kill you. Bro, I really don't want to see this right now." He gave me one of those long soap opera stares that happen right before a commercial break, then walked his phone to me, "Look." My blood shot through the roof to the point I damn near cracked Gunna's phone, squeezing it so tight. I didn't want to, but I needed to, so I pressed play.

"Buss down thotiona. Buss down thotiona on the dead locs." *Blueface played while a light skin nigga rockin' two French braids to the back with the sides faded, dipped in Chanel from the shoes up, Crip walked with my brotha's chain on.*

The boy stopped Crip walking and looked at the camera. *"Check it. This Lazy Loc, Rose City Crip bangin' and I'm a be real with you, Cuz." Somebody passed him a blunt. He hit it then continued, "No lie, the best weed out right now hands down this Juice that I'm smoking courtesy of the big homie, "hit the weed again*

"Cuz dispensaries ain't even got this, and it has been out over ten years. Anybody that knows Davontae Stokes AKA Lil Juice tell 'em the chain starting at fifty stacks and going up five by the day."

A group of niggas in the background threw their sets up.

I stood up, tossed the homie's phone, and voiced my anger, "These bitch niggas got me fucked up."

"Got you fucked?" TJ hopped off the couch, "Nigga they got Murda Gang fucked up," he stood silent, looking from face to face making sure everyone felt the same, "If one of us do something, the gang gets the blame. Gas Team ain't gon' give me a pass 'cause Gunna beat on Pusha, they coming for us."

TJ's words hit me something hard. It sounded dead on some of the ghetto gospel Gunna's known for preaching but coming from TJ fucked my head up.

I'd felt we hadn't been moving as a team since Omar died, but the passion in TJ's voice had gotten the whole room's attention leading me to believe we were coming together as one.

Chapter 14
Juice

Two weeks had flown by without one nigga dropping that mattered, and only two shootouts out of the five we'd been in mattered, and they were both with Drama Gang, which really fucked with me. The look on JoJo's face when he shot not only forced my hand but hurt me as well. I wanted him to believe me so bad every shot I threw had pained more and more, and I only threw 'em to back him off me and save Breonna.

We'd been walking out of Benihana after a lil date night Breonna and I had been on.

Breonna had gotten so scared she wanted to close the curtains on our lil situationship, but after copping us a nice townhouse in Vancouver along with a new model Kia for her, that thought died.

After spending a whole week with Breonna, I got the drop on the bitch nigga I spent my life waiting to kill, and the intel came from jail.

"This bitch nigga actually think he can get out become a Muslim and all his problems gon' die?" Gunna questioned every Friday was on that rug barefoot beggin' the nigga Allah for forgiveness. At least that's what O-Dawg told me." I explained.

Me and my twin demon were sitting in a rental he'd gotten in some bitch name down the street from the Mosque waiting for hat bitch nigga Freeze to walk out them doors.

"You know this one gon' bring out niggas who ain't held a gun since before we were born and was able to escape their enemies, with Islam." My brodie preached while turning off Moneybag yo and turning on Finesse 2 Tymes.

A chill feeling drifted through my body the second the beat came.

This must be how my brotha felt hearing 2 Pac.

Finesse 2 Tymes spoke that real true-to-life street shit only niggas really in the field would understand.

I relaxed in my seat while Gunna inhaled the exotic weed.

"Huh, Blood." He handed me the blunt.

I took one pull just to relax my nerves in hopes of dropping my anxiety level.

"You good blood?" He asked after I shot the blunt back so fast.

I covered my mouth while I coughed and spoke slow, "I wanna feel every bit of this shit gang. From the minute we bounce out to every step it takes to get the bitch nigga. I'm a stand over that nigga and dump at least ten in his face in front of his punk ass family."

"And anybody who don't like it could suffer the same treatment. And that's on the gang." Bro threw the set up.

We sat in the car so long waiting on the Jumah service to end Gunna fell asleep. I'd been so over-anxious, I don't even think I blinked more than twice in the last hour.

"Get up!" It's time." I tapped Gunna a few times.

He let out a long yawn, stretched his arms, and cracked his neck, "You ready, blood?"

I nodded, then pulled the beanie I'd been rockin over my face transforming that mothafucka into a ski mask, and then I checked the clip in my 40 cal.

Thirty-one if I'm added the one up top.

We slid out on demon time with one agenda. Crush Freeze, and neither one of us cared who died in the process.

Butterflies did circles, scrambling all in my stomach. The feeling I'd felt with every step had been parallel to what I'd felt seconds prior to my first body.

My eyes zeroed in on the door where people begin to come out of.

"Blood, we probably shouldn't have parked so far," Gunna stated the obvious.

I stopped for a second to take a deep breath, then sped walked.

The lot had been so packed cars were parked all on the side of the street.

"There he goes with that fat bitch," Gunna informed.

I saw the nigga I hated more than I ever hated anyone talking to some lil girl who looked no older than twelve years old. I thought of that day some real suckas shot at me with my daughter and bounced out, throwing shots, not caring who they hit. I thought about sparing him for the sake of his kid and all the kids who were out but that video popped in my head of the hoe nigga Lazy talking 'bout smoking on my dead brotha, then I ran across the street to send my bro some company.

"Alphonzo!" I wanted everyone there to know who had put their lives in danger.

Boca! Boca! Boca! Boca! Boca! Boca!

Me and Gunna ran side by side, moving the crowd, not caring who we hit.

"Call the cops," someone yelled.

"I'm over here, blood." Gunna tip-toed through the parking lot.

"Ahhh! Not my baby."

My ears had gotten pierced by the screams a mother shouted after their child had gotten shot, reminding me of my mother's screams the night my brotha had gotten shot dead in front of us both.

I damn near got hit by a couple of cars that were smashin' out in the hope of escaping the wraith of a possessed soul.

"Where the fuck this bitch at?" I stepped in the lot, watching the crowd move while Gunna threw shots.

A man dressed in a Men's Warehouse looking saw me and put his hand, "Brotha, I ain't been active in ten years cuz."

Boca!

"Don't smuz me, Crab," Gunna banged on 'em throwin' up the set then dropped another one in the dude.

I didn't even notice the homie creep up on me and score an easy lay-up.

The parking lot had been damn near empty, and it seemed like Freeze had just vanished.

"You gon' disrespect Allah cuz!"

My head swung in the direction the voice had come from and gotten greeted with a surprise at the surprise party I threw.

Boca! Boca! Boca! Boca!

I got low, trying not to get hit. I'd seen Gunna run and hide behind one of the few parked cars in the lot, and then I followed suit.

"This crab ass nigga came prepared," Gunna fumed.

"He better sleep and shower with it," I spoke through clenched teeth.

The shots stopped then I heard feet shuffling'.

I rose up to find a stocky bald nigga headed towards the building and chased behind, bustin' and not caring.

Boca! Boca!

I ran to the side after some bitch nigga shots were thrown my way, then I got back in route, and that bitch nigga had been about fifteen feet away.

Boca! Boca! Boca! Boca!

"Ugh Fuck! Cuz." He grunted after the last shot slapped his back, knockin' him close to the door.

I walked while he crawled on his stomach towards the door. I wanted to salvage every second of his death.

"Where my chain, bitch ass nigga?"

He laughed, "Lil Juice."

Honk! Honk!

"Po-po a few blocks down, blood. We gotta go!" Gunna shouted.

In that split second, I turned my head. By the time I looked at Freeze, the door to the Mosque had opened, and two people were draggin' Freeze inside.

Boca! Click!

"Fuck!" I spat after letting a whole thirty go and only hittin the nigga that I'd come for once.

I ran straight to the car, jumped in the backseat, and then we scratched off.

Sirens rang from behind, getting louder by the second. Sirens that were coming from in front of us rang out from afar.

"Blood, we gon' have to beat 'em on feet. They're coming at us from both angles.

I knew he'd been speaking the truth. Going to jail never worried me but going to jail without my brotha's chain and Freeze still breathing was something I wouldn't allow.

"A'ight. Call that bitch and tell her the car got stolen and she needs to report that bitch," I said.

"The bitch getting' a text, then I'm a bend a few blocks and gon' bounce out to figure it out, bro." Gunna sent a text off the pre-paid phone, then cut the car lights out, hit a few blocks. We parked between cars, turned our ski masks back to beanies, and slid out.

"We gon' creep low and look for a dark spot with no cars in the driveway," Gunna said.

We ran as fast as our legs would let us while being crouched down.

The drugs started getting the best of me. I'd gotten out of breath halfway down the block.

"Oh, shit, gang look." I pointed out.

My heart skipped a beat the moment I saw cops about a block and a half ahead of us.

"It's a gutta right here. We can drop the burners and move a lil."

"Lay down."

We dropped the heats off in the gutta then laid flat on the concrete. Lucky for us, the car sped past us. We ran block after block, and my legs were killing me to the point, I had to stand up for a bit to loosen my shit. We found an apartment complex and hid in a bando for a few hours. Gunna called TJ, and he actually came through in the clutch for us.

Marcellus Allen

Chapter 15
Freeze

It had been a week since that bitch nigga Lil Juice pulled that coward move with one of his bitch ass homeboys disrespecting my religion and disrespecting Crip'n, which happens to be the two things in my life I take seriously.

The Imam felt I'd put too many lives in danger and didn't want me anywhere in the Mosque. Then to make shit more fucked up, a lil girl had gotten killed, an older brotha who had changed his life over and stopped bangin' had gotten killed on the tenth-year anniversary of giving his life to Allah.

Fatimah threatened to take Aaliyah and leave the state, and that shit really fucked with me.

"What's crackin', loc?" I greeted all the homies with the signature Crip shake.

We were all at Trey's spot in Beaverton, and we were all ready to get shit crackin'.

"We just in here putting shit together, cuz. The lil slob was starting to get disrespectful in the worst way. Shot up a Mosque and killed my baby momma, cuz. On Crip, he gotta go," Trey expressed with a look in his eyes I hadn't seen in a while.

"I know where his momma stays," Cash blurted out.

From a street perspective, murkin' the bitch nigga's momma is a fair exchange for all the coward shit he'd been pulling, but I wasn't sure Allah would forgive me for killing an innocent woman. I knew pressing the button would make me just as guilty as pulling the trigger.

"Naw, we can't do a nigga's moms like that. We gotta keep this shit in the streets," I stated, knowing niggas would be conflicted about my stance on the whole situation. However, being a man of faith, lines had to get drawn.

"What you mean we can't go that far?" Forty spat as he hopped out of his seat. "That weak ass nigga killed the homie's baby mom, shot up the Mosque, and hit you in the back."

He had a compelling argument, but I couldn't give the ok for some Mexican Cartel shit. I already had to live with killing a pregnant woman who'd been innocent in the whole beef.

"All we gotta do is find out who his bitch is or any of his bitch's sports," Cash said while pouring a cup of Lean.

I have never been with all that social media shit because all people on them social sites do is fake stunt and dry snitch, and I'm not for either of them. Only niggas who gon' know the dirt I did are the niggas with me and the victims that I did it to.

We chopped it up for close to an hour trying to put something together but without an address on any of them marks, and there'd been only one way to go. Purge.

Five deep in a caravan, lurkin' with C-Bo playing out the car speakers on a mission to drop something.

We just filled the tank up for the second time, Cuz," Problem whined while driving.

"Cuz, I ain't going to rest until I put a nigga to sleep, and that's on Top Gun," I vowed. "Let me get that stick." I reached.

"Ok, cuz back." Forty handed me a Sherm dipped cigarette.

I needed to relax my nerves and focus on dropping my enemies. There'd been too much on the line for me to be hiding out with my tail tucked.

I took a long pull of the wet stick then handed it to Cash. "What's the most crackin' club?"

"Fuck, the club Mozzy is performing at the Roseland tonight. I know it's gon' be a lot of niggas to smoke," Trey stated.

The more wet I inhaled, the less I cared who my bullets touched.

"Aye, Cuz, who's red Beamer is that?" Trey asked.

I looked at the plates and knew exactly who's car it belonged to. My whole beef with Lil Juice is over their leader.

"Look, cuz. Let me and Problem out at the corner, and y'all block the drive-thru exit," I directed as we pushed down MLK Blvd, zoning out on the tinted out red Beamer in the McDonald's parking lot.

"Let's get these niggas, cuz." Problem put on his *Scream* mask.

I pulled my hoodie down and bounced out in pouring down rain, creepin' to our prey.

The Beamer had been stuck between two cars in the drive-thru. We waited until Trey blocked the exit, then we sprinted across the street and got it crackin'.

There'd been a lady hanging out of the drive-through window, handing whoever had been in the Beamer their order as I got up on 'em.

I gave Problem a quick head nod, then we ran up on the passenger side and got to knockin' at that bitch.

"Rose City Crip, Cuz!" I banged the set.

Boca! Boca! Boca! Bloaw! Bloaw! Boca! Boca!

Skirrrt!

The driver tried smashin' out the drive-thru from one side, but he hit the car in front of 'em.

"Hit Squad, Blood!" Jimmy banged as he hoped out the Audi that had been behind the Beamer flamin' shit.

Boca! Boca! Boca! Boca! Bloaw! Bloaw!

I knew I couldn't fade the baby chop Jimmy sprayed at us, so I threw a few shots while running towards the van. I dove in some bushes, looked over my shoulder, and saw my nigga stretched in the middle of the street, still holding his smack with holes in his face and body.

The Beamer smashed out and rolled over my nigga's body, and then I swissed cheesed that bitch from the bushes, causing the driver to wreck into a car flying down the street.

The shots from the other side stopped, and that's when I took full advantage.

Boca! Boca! Boca! Boca!

"Where you slob niggas at now?"

"Right here, blood." Fame came out the backseat of the Audi dumpin' something serious.

Boca! Boca!! Click!

The first time in my life I didn't count my bullets while blowing, I run out of shells.

"What's crackin, Cuz?" Forty came through and saved the day.

Boca! Boca! Boca! Boca!
I ran to the van while the homie back pedaled, servin' them suckas until we were both safe.
Then more shots rang out from behind us.

Chapter 16
Juice

For the past week, I'd been at Gunna's spot laying low, pissed at myself for letting that bitch nigga Freeze slip from my grip. The innocent people who'd been killed in the process didn't mean shit to me. They made a choice to be on the wrong side of the gun. There wasn't a person in the city of Portland who didn't know I wanted Freeze dead, but that's why it fucked me up to watch the news and see they had no suspects named in the whole shit.

"You know them niggas gon' try to come down hard blood," Gunna advised from the driver seat.

We were pushing down MLK Boulevard about to get a bite to eat when shit got real.

"Blood, what's that?" Gunna pointed at the action happening ahead of us.

I gripped the Mac 11 that sat on my lap and knew by the shape of the nigga bussin' at the Audi who it had been.

"Get up on 'em, gang." I pulled the stick out the drizzy, making sho' it had been stuffed.

Gunna hit the gas then slowed down across the street from McDonald's.

A red Beamer who I knew belonged to Breeze had been wrecked into a puck-up truck. Some white hillbilly-looking mu-fucka had been standing outside of the truck screaming.

"Blood, that's my relly's shit," Gunna shouted while parking.

I bounced out in the pouring rain to find the boy Problem on the ground crushed, and I mean crushed literally. The back tire to the Beamer had been next to his caved-in chest, defining the meaning of getting crushed.

I see the nigga that I spent the last decade dying to kill, hopping in a caravan behind his homie and running towards that bitch, letting shots go.

Boca! Boca! Boca! Boca! Boca! Boca! Boca!!

The van started swervin' crazy in and out of lanes, barely missing cars that were passing while shells from the Mac slapped every inch of the back end of the van.

I hopped around, dodging cars coming towards me, causing a huge traffic jam making cars crash while trying to nail my target.

Boca! Boca! Boca! Clack!

"Fuck!" I spat after my smack jammed.

"Blood, the Boys are coming!" Gunna yelled.

I watched Freeze slip from my grip once again, then hopped in the car with Gunna, and scratched off with our freedom.

Chapter 17
Juice

Shit had gotten so hot me and Gunna had to park and hit up a telly downtown.

"Blood, that shit was brazy on the gang. That shit was like so G.T.A type shit. Lil Breeze was slumped in drives seat with a dead bitch in his lap." Gunna explained being extra as always.

I sat in a chair at the table sippin' out of a Sprite bottle filled with more Lean than soda, still pumped with adrenaline from the smoke session we just had.

"How the fuck that fuck nigga keep escaping a kill's grip?" I stressed while handing Gunna the bottle.

"God must want you to stand over him." He took a fat gulp then handed it back to me.

I took a gulp," Think so?" I looked up at bro.

He stopped pacing and stared at me, "Why else, you think?"

I let that shit soak in while texting Breonna, woozy off the Lean after realizing I hadn't hit nothin' in over a week. Twenty minutes later, a knock at the door low-key spooked a nigga.

"Blood, I ain't ask for no room service." Gunna gripped his glizzy, then walked to the door and checked the peephole.

"It's Jessie. You text her?"

I looked at my phone, and then my palm slapped my forehead after noticing I'd been texting with Jessie, not Breonna.

"So, you finally tapped in for some real nigga dick?" Gunna opened the door.

She looked good as fuck with her hair wrapped in a bun, wearing nothing but a tall tee and Retro ten's.

She pushed past Gunna and stopped in front of me, "You need a ride home, Davontae, right?"

"Yep." I smirked, forgetting how high I'd been 'till I stood up and wobbled a lil then caught my balance and followed her lead.

"You make it here quick."

Gunna looked from me to her, then shook his head. "I wouldn't pass it up either, gang." He dapped me.

I didn't pay his words any attention. I just followed her out. She ain't waste no time. The second we stepped in her crib, it was on. Under that tall tee, she had nothing but a beautiful body.

"Thirsty, Pappi?"

I watched her bare checks dribble to the kitchen as she grabbed a bottle of Patron, filled two shot glasses, and handed one to me.

"What we toastin' to?" I couldn't take my eyes off her body.

"You tearing this pussy up."

Our glasses kissed, then we downed our shots, took two more shots, and then she led me to her room.

I got a lil choked up seeing pictures of Naughty on the dresser and wall.

She started suckin' on my neck while loosening my belt.

"There's nobody she would want with you besides me."

The guilt began getting hold of my mental, making me feel conflicted until Jessie dropped down and took me in her mouth.

I felt a litter of spit drenched my dick.

"Slurp, slurp."

Just like that, she sucked it off. She must have felt my guilt making my dick go limp because she sped the motion up then ticked my peephole with the tip of her tongue, making my legs wobble.

"Hol' up, Pappi." She got up, ran to her drawer, grabbed a peppermint, popped it in her mouth, and then started toppin' me with the peppermint in her mouth, pushing whatever emotional guilt feeling I felt far from my mind.

"Oh shit, Fuck!" I placed a hand on the back of her head.

She stopped and looked up at me, "I don't need no help suckin' dick, so take your hand off my head."

I followed her command and let her do her thang til I shot in her mouth. She swallowed it then sucked it back hard.

"Damn mami, you got the best head ever. On the gang."

"Oh, I know. It ain't over just yet, Pappi."

I stripped down to nothing and hopped in her soft fluffy queen size bed.

She hopped on top and slid down my pole, turned around, and slow rode me while I watched that ass bounce every ounce of cum out of me.

Marcellus Allen

Chapter 18
Juice

Ring, ring, ring.
"Jessie, get yo phone," I said, still asleep and in a groggy tone. I wiped the cold from my eyes and found myself alone in the bed. "Ahh!" I stretched, then hopped out of the bed and answered my phone.

"Big bro, I'm sorry. I should never have doubted you." Sincerity mixed with the tears. My head made the regret seem real, but him trying to line me at the club and then trying to knock my head off had played in my mind on repeat.

I gripped the phone like it had been a pistol as anger and hurt boiled in my blood.

"I'm 'pose to just sweep everything under the rug that happened?" My teeth clenched as I fought back the feeling of letting my emotions show.

"What would you have done in my shoes?'

"What made you believe me?" I asked the billion-dollar question.

"That bitch ass crab nigga crab steppin' with yo brotha's chain on had me hot ass fuck, blood. On Naughty's grave, I swore to put that nigga down." The pain in his voice damn near matched mine.

Hearing lil bro put it on my bitch's grave sent a shock through my body like hearing the words on Omar's grave.

"I got something for you, but we need to Facetime."

I hopped on the Facetime and couldn't help but smile at the nigga who'd been tied up in the trunk of JoJo's car.

"Where you niggas at?" I started getting dressed.

"Pappi good morning." Jessie stepped in carrying a plate filled with breakfast foods.

"Who that blood?"

"Just drop the addy, and I'll be there." I hung up before he found out I'd been smashin' Jessie on the low.

About an hour and some change later, Gunna and I pulled up to his ride to the location JoJo had given me.

"You sho' he ain't tryin' a line a nigga?" Gunna asked the question that had been beating my head up since answering the phone.

"I honestly believe the nigga. But just in case shit gets out of hand, circle the block one more time, gang."

We circled the block twice, then backed in just in case we had to drop shells and smash out.

"Blood, I'm a be real," Gunna stared deep in my eyes and kept it a buck. "I know how you feel 'bout the lil nigga, but if anything seems off, I won't hesitate to blow my gun."

I didn't have any response for bro. I just hopped out and got to it.

We stepped into a garage covered with plastic all over the floor and strapped to a chair had been the bitch nigga who went by the name Lazy Loc.

The boy had two black eyes, scraps, scratches, and bruises all over his face. Blood dripped from his mouth, staining his shirt and jeans while a couple of teeth lay at his feet.

Ghost stood next to JoJo, looking extra tough like a nigga was doing security for Suge Knight.

Whatever doubt I had about lil bro, it all died after seeing his face light up when he saw me.

"The bitch nigga said Freeze got it," JoJo informed, dappin' me with a G-Hug.

I felt myself getting upset all over again, and I had to calm myself down and appreciate what lil brodie had brought me.

"Well, he gon' have to drop the addy," Gunna stated.

"We done beat everything out the nigga," JoJo reported while Ghost nodded with an extra hard look on his face.

"Let me see the nigga's phone." I got the phone from JoJo.

I tried getting to the contacts in the phone, but they'd beat the bitch nigga so bad the phone wouldn't even recognize his face for close to thirty minutes later.

All the Rose City Crip niggas were in his phone except the one who mattered the most, but I knew just who to Facetime to get shit started.

"When the homies get to you slob niggas," Lazy's words slurred, crackin' us all up as bloody slobber dripped off of his busted lips.

"By that time, you gon' be a dead loc," Ghost joked for the first time ever.

"I ain't know blood had a sense of humor," Gunna said.

"He even surprises me sometimes, and I'm with him every day," JoJo confessed.

"You like crab steppin' with real niggas chains on, huh?" I said my lil disrespectful shit just to get under the fuck nigga's skin as I called his bitch ass homie up.

I sat the screen on Lazy's beat-up face while we waited for Trey to answer.

"Cuz what happened to you?" Trey answered on the third ring, sounding like he'd really been concerned.

I put the screen on us so the sucka ass fuck nigga could see the demons who had his bitch ass homeboy held hostage.

"Where my chain at hoe ass nigga." I taunted.

"You doing this for that weak ass chain or yo bitch ass slob brotha the homie smoked in yo face cuz."

Looking at the fuck nigga smirk at me, low-key fucked with me, but before I could even speak, lil bro spoke his truth.

"Fuck you and all you crab niggas. You faggots killed my pregnant sister, so when I catch yo momma, baby momma, or anybody who matters to you, I'm doing 'em dirty, blood," JoJo vowed through anger.

"You already lost a baby momma, so drop a hunnid stacks, bro's chain, and Freeze's addy. We just might let yo nigga live."

Trey chuckled at Gunna's request. "Cuz, he ain't makin it out alive."

"You right," I cut in, then fell through on what I meant.

Boca! Boca! Boca! Boca!

Blood splashed on my shirt, jeans, and shoes, plus drenched the phone. Not one of the niggas with me moved a muscle. We were numb to dead bodies, and a dead opp only added to the scoreboard.

I let the blood drip off the phone, and to my surprise bitch ass Trey had still been on the phone, so I decided to fuck with him a lil.

"How it feels to lose you baby momma and homie to the hands of the same nigga?"

"That's fucked up." Ghost adlibbed.

I deaded the call and moved on to the next mission.

Chapter 19
Freeze

"Alphonzo, where do you think you're going?" Fatimah stressed from the bed.

I'd gotten caught packing a bag of clothes, cash, and a pistol. I needed to protect my family, and the bitch ass slob nigga, Lil Juice, had been moving real recklessly by killing innocent people and not caring anything about it all in hopes of getting to me over some shit from my past life.

I sat on the bed next to my wife and gave her my truth. "Fatimah, I gotta put an end to all this chaos that's been going on. I can't afford to lose you or Aaliyah to this lil knuckle head."

"Alphonzo, I'm not doing another prison term. I can't, and I won't put that kind of pressure on Aaliyah again."

I knew the tears were there before I even heard her sniffling! I knew looking at her would emotionally kill me, so I continued packing with my back to her while I spoke.

"I would never put us through that again. I regretted every day I couldn't spend with you."

"Why can't we just move?"

"Cause these problems."

"Look at me, Lonzo." She hopped off the bed then made me face her, "Earlier, you said this knuckle head. Who were you talking about?"

I knew I'd slipped the second I'd said the words 'this knucklehead', but I figured she didn't catch it since she'd kept talking.

"You're just going to ignore me? What's supposed to happen with us, huh? What about your daughter? What am I supposed to tell her?"

Every question hit me like a knife to the heart only because I knew the chances of me making it back in one piece wasn't as likely as I hoped she'd believed.

"Daddy, where are you going?" Aaliyah's voice grabbed every ounce of my attention.

I walked up to my daughter, held her hand, and walked back to her room.

I sat at the foot of her bed with her, just staring into her eyes, not knowing how to explain my reason for leaving.

"Are you and mommy getting a divorce?" her words had hit me like a ton of bricks.

"Naw never that, baby girl."

"Are you moving out?"

"No, not one bit. Daddy just got some stuff to handle, and I'll be gone for a few days," I gave the edited version.

How could I even think of breaking my princess's heart with the truth? As much as I hated lying to her, I had to do everything in my power to protect her and shield her from all negative forces formed by Satan.

Nothing had hurt more than seeing the upset faces on Fatimah and Aaliyah's faces, but as a man, I had business to handle, and I wasn't coming back home until it had gotten handled.

Chapter 20
Juice

Damn near a week went by, and I wasn't any closer to Freeze's where-about, and the shit started really stressing me the fuck out. Then to add insult to injury, we were out of work, and the streets were fienin'.

Lil bro suggested we take a load off at the club, but I didn't feel like clubbin'. There'd been too much going on to be outside playing and shit, but due to it being lil bro's birthday, I fell through the club to show JoJo a lil love.

"This mafucka lit blood," Gunna said as me him and Mask stepped into the club.

"There he goes right there, gang." Mask pointed at JoJo's section.

I'd already noticed my Drama Gang niggas, but my eyes had been scanning the room for opps and any nigga who wanted to inhale a gram of smoke.

I felt every eye in the spot follow us to JoJo's section.

Who the fuck invited this nigga?" Faith yelled, then hopped off Breeze's lap and ran down on me but stopped a few feet from me.

"Bitch I ain't explaining myself again," I stepped up on her with both fists balled. "Breeze, get yo bitch."

She must have sensed me seconds from taking her off of the face of Earth because she turned all the way down.

"I can't just sit around and party with the nigga who killed my best friend," she grabbed her purse then stopped in JoJo's face," I don't know how you can be around a nigga who killed yo sister."

"I told you he ain't kill my sister. Now apologize to my big bro and calm yo ass down." JoJo checked.

She dismissed everything he said with a hand jester then stomped out.

"Blood, thank you," Breeze dapped me, "I need a break from her ass, my nigga. But how you holding up?"

"I'm making it." I downplayed my emotional state.

I couldn't let a nigga outside of Murda Gang know my mental state.

Hit-Squad niggas were alright with me to a degree. I'll never forget the facts, though. Those facts are my brotha helped put Hit-Squad on the map, and after that bitch nigga Freeze killed him, not one Hit-Squad nigga dropped a single body on my brotha's behalf. That shit never sat right with me. Plus, I did murk Marcel without an ounce of regret in my soul.   "What you smirking at, nigga?" Mask took me out of my own thoughts.

"Probably that bitch nigga Shotta." Black pointed to the section the remainder of Murk Unit niggas were.

My focus swung to the section Shotta, and three other unknown suckas were just living it up, having the time of their life with a couple of thotties.

"Lil bro, let them bitch niggas live." Jimmy gave a shot at keeping the peace.

Jimmy's words had let me know he didn't know shit about the beef between my niggas and the Murk Unit, or if he did, he must have forgotten. I had my own way of going about things.

"No, this crab ain't 'bout to walk up in my section." JoJo stood in front of the velvet rope, and Ghost stood right next to the nigga.

"Bro, we don't want no smoke," Shotta tried copping a plea while two of his homies stood there looking tough.

Whop!

"The smoke a never clear." Gunna banged after smackin' Shotta with a fifth of Henny.

"Ahh!" Shotta screamed after blood gushed out of his greasy ass forehead.

Everybody in the club started moving around. Bitches were screaming and trying to run for safety while bottles and fists were being thrown.

"Cuz what's crackin'?" One of the unknown suckas pulled his pants up and got in his fighting stance, then JoJo dope fiend him, and Ghost hopped in.

"Cuz I can't win this one." The other nigga ran through the crowd knocking people over.

I joined Gunna and Mask and stampeded designer shoes all over Shotta's face and body.

"Break that shit up!" Some big penitentiary buff ass bouncer yelled as he pushed his way towards us.

"Blood, I know you ain't tryin' to die for this job." Breeze pressed a .380 against the bouncer's chin.

The bouncer froze up and raised both hands in the air, "I ain't dying for two hundred dollars a night...but the owner did call the cops, homie."

All I needed to hear were the words cops, and I was gone. I couldn't afford to go to jail without killing Freeze.

After everything died down, I made my way home. I hadn't seen Breonna in over two weeks, so I expected an argument or at least having to fuck all the naggin' out of her, but to my surprise, she'd just been happy to see me.

"Have you eaten?" she asked while wiping down the kitchen counter.

"Naw, but I'm hungry, though." I flopped down on the living room couch.

"Good because I cooked spaghetti and garlic bread." She whipped me up a plate and then brought it to me.

I should have been fuckin' with her.

We had a quiet lil dinner, just us catching up while watching the Blazer's play. Just sitting and chopping it up with her had me feeling like I could actually build a life with her.

For the past two weeks, I'd been in the crib with Bre, letting things in the streets die down. It seemed like the bitch nigga, Alphonzo, just fell off the face of the Earth. I couldn't get a line on him or any of his bitch ass homeboys, and had it not been for Bre convincing Toyah to let Lisa spend the day with me, I probably would have caught a senseless body.

"Did you have fun today, baby?" I asked as I parked in the complex Toyah lived in.

"Yup. I had a lot of fun, daddy. But next time, can Ashley come with us?"

That question had hit me hard because I hated the position it had put me in. Nothing had hurt more than not being able to give my children what they wanted, but Lisa had been too young to understand the truth, so I'd gave her what I felt had been appropriate for a child her age.

"We'll have to see how her mom feels about it. Ok?"

"Okay, daddy. But since she's my sister, maybe I should ask."

I couldn't help but smile. She had her mother's ways when it came to being persuasive and getting what she wanted.

"Well, next time when we go out, I'll make sure you call and see if Ashley gets to hang out with us." I hit the locks on the door, then started to get out. I was stopped by Lisa's voice.

"Daddy, before I go, can I have some money?" I pulled out a knot and started searching for a couple of small bills, but then I thought about how long it's been since I'd gotten the chance to hang out with her.

Tomorrow ain't promised.

I peeled off a couple of hundred-dollar bills, then pulled out every dollar under a twenty I had and made her day.

"This is all for me? WOW! Daddy, I'm really a baller now."

I couldn't stop laughing while I watched her organize the money that I'd just given her and then stuff it in her Hello Kitty purse.

"Juice, I need to holla at you, bro," Rocky said as soon as me and Lisa stepped in.

I had an idea of what he wanted to discuss, but I really didn't care to. However, due to the nature of the info that he was giving me, I decided to hear him out.

"Baby, me and Rocky gon' talk while you tell yo momma about all the fun we had." I gave Lisa a hug then kissed her on the forehead.

"Sup, my nigga." I dapped Rocky.

"I need a re-up, bro," he got straight to it.

I knew he needed more work, and I didn't have an issue with giving it to him. It was just my well had run dry.

"What you tryin' to get?" I asked, not wanting to lose any clientele.

"What's the price of a whole one?"

I hated not having work while having clientele in need. Hearing Rocky asking for a brick just let me see a small portion of the money I was missing out on.

"Look, bro. You be looking after my daughter when I'm not able to, so off the strength of that, I'm a plug you, fam. Just give me time to put a few things together."

"What the fuck y'all talkin 'bout?" Toyah yelled as she rushed into the living room.

Normally, I would have checked her for all that yelling at a nigga, but I had bigger fish to fry.

"Nothin' but thank you for letting Lisa spend the day with me. I gave her a hug, then dapped Rocky and blew that joint before she could get all in my mix.

Marcellus Allen

Chapter 21
Juice

"Gang, we gotta figure something out because I'm all out of work, and my lil niggas are getting hungry and reckless," Gunna said while twistin' a wood.

We were posted at Gunna's spot trying to figure out our next play. The whole gang had been in attendance, but the pressure seemed to be placed on me.

I knew what needed to be done, but I didn't have the information needed to put the play in motion.

"The work I been coppin' from Breeze been moving easy," TJ confessed.

I have never been the type to hold a nigga back but hearing TJ admitting to coppin' work from a nigga, I knew who couldn't fill half the order Jaxx had been supplying seemed a lil off.

"So, you ain't think anybody else wanted to eat?" Mask questioned from the couch across from the one I sat on.

TJ hopped out of his seat and defended his sneaky tactics." Ain't' nobody question Juice when O-Dawg was feeding him for hits we-"

I sprang to my feet and stepped in his face and checked him. "Because everything I did, I did it for the gang. Now you got something to say about that?"

I stood in that nigga's face praying he said the wrong thing so he could become one less nigga I had to stress about.

"Blood y'all need to relax with all that shit. We all family ain't nothin' but gang in here." Gunna tried defusing the issue.

"Fa real." Flash hopped off the couch and stood in between me and TJ. "We need to figure out how we gon' get that bougie nigga Jaxx."

I stared at TJ dead in his eyes as my hand eased towards my waist, itching to take his life. I still felt some type of way about him leaving Omar to die in the street like my bro was an opp.

"It seems like this nigga always feels the need to throw my name around," I growled without letting one eye leave TJ's face.

TJ must have known what had been best because he took a few steps back before expressing his weak ass emotions.

"I'm just saying if a nigga expects me to be setting around starving waiting to be fed, they got another thing coming."

I felt him because I wouldn't let near nigga block my grind, but his lil rants were starting to get a lil too hostile for me to ignore. I made a mental note to myself to keep an eye on him.

"I feel you, gang." I dapped him, lowering the level of tension that controlled the room then we put a play in place to eliminate all our enemies and get rich in the process.

Life just didn't seem the same without my brotha's chain around my neck. I'd been on edge going back and forth with the only niggas who I knew had my back no matter the odds. I thought about Omar and what he would want for us, then I thought about if I had been in TJ's shoes, what made the most sense.

If I was him, I'd leave with my life, so I was able to avenge my nigga.

"If we gon' get this nigga Jaxx, we gon' need something that matters to him." I paused for a few seconds to look in each set of eyes in the room to make sure everyone had been on the same page.

The hunger in everyone's eyes had been evident. All I'd seen were a pack of beasts who were anxious to feast.

"The best way to get through to the nigga would be through his family," TJ suggested.

"But he so cautious, he probably knows every neighbor's car on his block," Flash said.

I knew the place we'd been meeting that scary nigga at wasn't where he laid his head. Anyone on his level moving the type of weight he moved lived far away from where he did business.

"O-Dawg locked up, and Twin is in the hospital, we can control the town with enough money and dope. We just gotta get to the money and dope," I said as I got the blunt from Gunna and inhaled the exotic weed. I could tell by the looks on everyone's faces that Twin being in the hospital had come as a shock to niggas.

We spent the next thirty minutes devising the perfect plan for lashin' Jaxx.

Chapter 22
Juice

"So, what am I to you?" Jessie asked low-key, causing a scene in the gas station's parking lot.

"We friends, right?" I tried playing it light.

I'd been ignoring all her calls and text since the last time we smashed, and the bitch had been blowing me up. It was just my luck that I happened to stop for gas and Woods and ran into Jessie while coming out of the store.

"Are you serious, Juice?" she questioned with her hands on her hips.

I gave a lil shoulder shrug which I ended up regretting the second I did it because it brought out a side of her that I'd never seen.

"No, Davontae," she got all in my face poking me with her finger while she called herself checkin' me. "You think I just fuck niggas to fuck just 'cause, huh? How many niggas you know that I gave some pussy?"

Outside of that one nice ass Salem nigga who'd been trickin' something crazy, I couldn't name another nigga that I'd seen her with.

"Be real, Jessie. This shit doesn't seem weird to you? Naughty was yo best friend!"

"Are you serious, Juice?" she shook her head. "Yes, I love Naughty, but-"

"Jessie, don't do it. You know what she meant to me," I threatened through clenched teeth.

No matter what Naughty and I had been going through prior to her death, I wouldn't ever let a soul speak down on my bitch. The look on Jessie's face had let me know she'd caught my drift.

"What y'all arguing about?"

Now I knew why she'd gotten all wide-eyed and froze up. I didn't need any more enemies than I already had. Plus, me and lil bro just got back good. Another gun bussin' with me had made more sense than busting at me.

I let out a light sigh as I turned around and greeted the homie with false excitement for seeing him.

"JoJo, what's good with bro?" I dapped him.

His energy had given away his suspicion. At least that's what I felt, or it could a been the guilt I had for fuckin' my bitch's best friend.

"Shit, I was just at sis's gravesite, dropping flowers off."

Just hearing lil bro say he was at my bitch's grave rattled my soul. It hurt me to the core not being able to stare into Naughty's eyes. To make shit heavier on me had been our last convo because she pleaded and begged me for peace, but all I had for her were death threats.

"You a strong lil nigga on the gang. I don't think I'll be able to visit her 'till I kill that bitch nigga Freeze." Anger dripped off of every word I'd just spoken.

"Well, I'm a let y'all two catch up. I gotta get ready for work." Jessie gave us each a hug then went on about her business.

"Blood, we have been out here huntin' for them hoes ass Rose City Crabs."

"You ain't the only one who been out here seeking revenge, but it seems like they just fell off the map, though," I honestly confessed.

"Well, them bitch ass Gas Team niggas been online talkin real greasy. The Flip nigga been on Facebook talkin' real high power." He handed me his phone, so I could see what the hype was about.

It wasn't anything outside of the normal shit-talking and wolfing on his gangsta, knowing damn well he couldn't inhale a whiff of the smoke I bring to a nigga.

I handed him his phone. "Man, damn. Niggas ain't put a soul in the sky for Jamar. The only thing them pussies did was drop a R.I.P. song."

"You know I wouldn't be a real nigga if I didn't let my big bro know what niggas out here doing feel me. But I gotta buss a couple moves blood." He dapped me then we went our separate ways.

My phone had been lighting up something serious on the console when I hopped in my shit. I saw hella unread text messages from Jessie along with a grip of missed calls, but only one had been worth replying to.

"What's up, Ma?" I pulled out of the gas station with no real destination.

"I haven't heard from you since Naughty's funeral, son. How are you holding up?"

No matter what went on in my life, I could never add stress to my momma's worries by being honest about my life.

I'm good, ma. Just taking it one day at a time."

"Well, I just called to check on you and let you know that Brittany is dropping Ashley off with me for the weekend, and my grandbaby really wants to see her dad, so..."

"I'm a be there fa' show. I'm a take her shoppin'."

"Davontae, slow down. Brittany made it clear that she doesn't trust you leaving with Ashley. I practically had to beg her to let me have some time with her, so I'm hoping you can come here and spend a few days with your daughter without any problems. Right?"

I felt my foot relax on the gas a lil as I began growing upset with the females in my life. I couldn't believe Britt would bring that fuck shit to my momma like I wasn't a good father. She knew exactly what I'd been fucked up about. My nigga had died, and one impulsive slap across her face erased everything we were.

Britt knew just who to go through to get to me. She knew I couldn't argue with my momma.

"I don't care if I gotta spend the weekend at yo house. I'm not missing out on any time I can spend with my babies," I caved for the sake of my child.

While I'd been listening to my momma preach the 'Good Word' to me, I pulled up to a stop light to find one of the greatest gifts I'd received in a while pull up beside me in a Camaro with the top dropped.

I hung up on my momma without notice and slyly slid out my car from the passenger seat, crept around my car, then I invited myself in the sucka's car. I hopped in the backseat and pressed my banga against the nigga's temple. I stopped him from rappin' to the song that played out of his sound system.

"Don't let me stop you. This that diss song you made calling niggas flunky and shit, right Pusha?"

"I mean, you heard it." He stretched his hand out while trying to save face.

"If you move an inch without my permission, I'ma blow yo top," I promised.

"You ain't finna buss yo gun on this busy ass street." He tried putting me to the test, but what he failed to realize was that I aced all my gun exams.

I noticed his phone ringing on the console and the pistol in his lap. I reached over, grabbed his pistol, sat it on the backseat, and then grabbed the phone off the console.

"Oh, shit, perfect time," I answered the Facetime call.

"Flip, my nigga, what's the triv?"

The look on his face could have been the emoji for defeat.

"Cuz, if anything happens-"

Boca! Boca!!

Pusha's head fell against the door as blood stained the dashboard.

"Save yo speech for the next Gas Team meeting. And make sho' y'all drop Pusha's album because dead rappers get the best promotion. Murda Gang over everything." I ended the call, wiped the phone off, tossed it in front of my car, hopped in my shit, and ran that bitch over as I scratched off laughing.

Chapter 23
Freeze

For the past two weeks, I'd been staying in a cheap telly downtown, only leaving to spin a few blocks. I heard Lil Juice and some of them lil niggas he be with were known to be at, but so far, I had unsuccessful trip after another, and the shit had frustrated me to the core. I hadn't seen or spoken to Fatimah or my daughter since I'd made the decision to leave, but I knew it had been only for the good. I'd been on my last line of patience with Lil Juice and his overzealous attempts on my life. I had to put a stop to it by all means.

I sat in a rented Civic down the street from where Lil Juice Momma stayed waiting to catch him slippin' like I did his brotha back in the day. For the past three days, I'd been driving down the block, parking in different areas of the street keeping an eye on his Momma's house but I hadn't seen shit besides some young sista who I'd guessed is Lil Juice's baby momma brought a cute lil brown skin girl through.

Watching Lil Juice's mother interact with the lil girl reminded me of seeing Aaliyah and my mom playing together.

"Now this ain't right. I gotta keep it in the streets." I voiced aloud to myself, letting Allah take control of my actions and force me to pull off as a black-tinted out Nissan parked in the driveway.

Naw, Lil Juice drives a Bentley, I thought as I bent the corner.

Marcellus Allen

Chapter 24
Juice

"Daddy, daddy!" Ashley shouted as she ran and jumped in my arms the moment my feet hit the front porch.

I hadn't seen her so long. I had to fight back tears of joy as I held my youngest child.

My momma and Britt stood at the door smiling from ear to ear, making me feel every ounce of regret that I felt after slappin' Britt. Had I known it would hurt my relationship with my child, then maybe I wouldn't have done it.

I looked at Britt and silently thanked her for allowing me to spend time with Ashley.

"Ok, baby, give mommy a hug before I go." Britt scooped Ashley up and pecked her cheeks a few times.

"Mommy, you're not gonna stay and play with us?"

"Not this time. I'm a let your grandma and daddy spend the weekend with ya." Britt killed Ashley's dreams of a family date.

"A'ight, I'll be here Sunday afternoon." Britt hugged my momma then headed to her car.

"Britt hol' up," I turned to Ashley. "Baby, go with yo grandma while I talk to ya momma."

The look in Britt's eyes made my soul cringe a bit. Not once since we'd been dealing with each other had I ever sensed any fear of being around me in her, but as she stood next to her car wide-eyed with a frightened look in her eyes, fearful of me is all I saw, and it fucked with me. Out of all the disloyal and deceitful bitches I dealt with, Britt had never been one of them. She'd always put me first.

"I got something for you and Ashley." I grabbed the Jan sport backpack from out the trunk of the car and gave it to her. "That's for you and Ashley."

She stared at me, batting her pretty brown eyes on me for a few seconds before expecting the backpack.

"Davontae, what's this?"

"That's fifty bands for you and my daughter. Open on account for her and save it for college or something."

A few seconds of silence flew by while we stared at each other. It's been a minute since we'd been in the same presence, so just as she'd stood there taking me in, I'd been doing the same to her.

She looked fine ass fuck standing there with her hair wrapped in a bun, rocking a long sundress that did a bad job of hiding her curves.

"Davontae, are you ok?"

"Yea, I'm good. It's just..." My mind drifted back to the night she'd caught me sniffin coke in her kitchen. "You know tomorrow ain't promised."

"I thought you were tryin' a buy back my forgiveness." She gave a lil smirk letting me know she'd been lowering her guard.

"Naw," I chuckled. "But I do apologize for my actions and what I did that night."

"I appreciate your apology, but-"

"It's all good, Britt. I just felt I owed you that because I was out of line that night. But I gotta go before Ashley get to trippin."

I turned to walk away, but her voice had stopped me.

"Davontae, how about you just bring her home on Sunday?"

I gave a head nod of approval then went inside.

Life had me so stressed sex couldn't even distract me, but after Toyah dropped Lisa off and I had both of my lil princesses with me, my whole attitude changed.

"Daddy, this person keeps calling you." Lisa handed me my phone.

I'd been baking cookies with Ashley while Lisa played on my phone, taking pictures of me in my baker's attire.

"Yea." I slapped the phone against my ear while leaning against the counter.

"Why haven't you returned any of my calls?"

The second I'd heard her voice, I regretted answering the phone.

"Jessie, I'm with my daughters right now."

"You couldn't just text me?"

I ended the call then blocked her. She'd become more stressful than she was a stress-relief, and I didn't need that shit while being with my daughters.

"Did I just hear you on the phone with Jessie? Naughty's friend Jessie?" my momma questioned as she stepped into the kitchen.

"Yea, why?" I handed my phone to Lisa, trying to avoid any eye contact with my mom.

She knew the type of nigga her and the streets raised me to be, but I would never use my voice to remind her. I just gave my focus to my children and enjoyed my time with them, but I couldn't help but feel my mother's eyes staring me down.

Chapter 25
Juice

I haven't had so much fun without killing a nigga since my nuts dropped but having daughters would do that to young killa. I spent the weekend doing all the stuff lil girls found fun except putting make-up or fingernail polish on me because real niggas don't do that weird shit. I hated having to deny my kids anything, but when Ashley tried putting that clear-coated paint on my nails, I had to draw the line, and I had no problem explaining it to her.

For a brief second, I'd forgotten about everything until Toyah came through and picked up Lisa, then reality sat in. I had Toyah help me put on my vest before she took Lisa home than I strapped up and went to drop Ashley off.

My phone started ringing as I started strapping Ashley in her car seat.

Unknown.

I instantly screened the call and continued putting Ashley in her seat. I stopped to admire how cute my baby had looked, sleeping so peacefully without a care in the world. At that moment, my mind had drifted to the last time I'd seen my brotha, and then I felt my anger rise thinking about the bitch nigga who robbed him of the privilege of becoming a father right on the street I stood on.

I closed the backdoor and looked to the side where I noticed a scandalous-looking nigga in a hoodie creeping towards me, causing my street nigga instincts to go into full drive as my hand slid to my waist and eased to Forty Cal off as I fell into demon mode.

"What's crackin, Cuz?" the nigga banged.

Boca! Boca! Boca! Boca!

I ducked between two parked cars, now knowing who the voice had belonged to, and rose up flamin' shit.

Boca! Boca! Boca! Boca!

I watched the bitch nigga try and retreat, running and hiding between parked cars but little did he know he tried me on the block I'd grew up on, so there's no way of escaping the inevitable.

The rain began slowing up, allowing heavy breathing and foot-steps to be heard. I got low and let my ears guide me.

I rose up and spun to my right just in time to catch the bitch nigga.

"Got ya, bitch," I taunted, then let it blow.

Boca! Boca! Boca!!!

"Ugh!" I grunted after the second shot slapped my back, send-ing me against a van while dropping my gun. "Fuck!" I looked around from the ground, low-key frightened for the first time since losing the realest nigga to stomp across Earth. I thought about my daughter in the car, lonely, and pulled myself to my feet.

The sounds of sirens were coming from afar. When I got to my feet, I saw a short, stocky-looking nigga hop in a Civic that was too clean to be a *stoley*. He scratched off, and then I saw a nigga crawl-ing towards me with blood drippin out the side of his neck.

Even with a vest on, the pain of receiving a shell stung, but after seeing the nigga's face who tried reuniting me with Omar, a shot of adrenaline hit me harder than a ten-year-old boy taking his first shot of Henny.

I snagged my gun off the ground, walked up on the nigga, and kicked him in the face.

"Ahh!" He cried out for help, but those cries fell on death's ears.

A devilish smirk made its way across my face. "Damn, now they gon' be saying flip got flipped." I pressed my foot against the blood leaked from his neck just to fuck with him before I sent him to watch Pusha perform his lil weak ass diss tracks, then I took a few steps back and closed his casket.

Boca! Boca!! Click!

"Thank God I ran outta shells 'cause now they can probably piece ya face back together." I let out a sinister laugh, then jogged to my car and took my daughter home.

Chapter 26
Freeze

The smell of gravy-smothered lamb chops shot up my nostrils the second I opened the front door. I moved past our well-cleaned living room and felt myself becoming warm-hearted after seeing pictures of my family and I throughout the living room and stopped a few feet shy of the kitchen.

Fatimah had been over the stove with her back to me draped in Muslim attire from the neck down. I walked up to her and wrapped my arms around her waist.

She inhaled my sent then rested her head on my chest, "I knew Allah would help my King find his way back to our palace."

"I realized it wouldn't be fair to put personal problems above us." I'd given only half-truths.

I only had one serious enemy, and if he wasn't dead or seri-ously paralyzed from the back shots I'd given him, he'd have to come and get me. I refused to allow my past to determine my future.

"Insha Allah." She replied, then turned around and gave me a real passionate kiss.

"Where's Aaliyah?" I slid from her grip and grabbed a bottle from the fridge.

"She'll be back tomorrow. She's with my mother, my king."

"Have you found a place we can live?"

The priceless smile that came across her face had told me all I needed to know.

After we ate, I helped her with the dishes then we watched *Love Jones,* which happens to be her favorite movie. Once the movie ended, we made love 'til daybreak.

Close to two months went by before the Imam felt safe, allow-ing my family and I back in the Mosque. And to be honest, I couldn't blame him for his concerns about my prior life. Innocent people were not only hurt, but also dead because a couple of young chumps wanted me dead for some shit that happened before they were even in the streets.

My black-on-black Escalade pulled into the Applebee's parking lot in downtown Salem where I'd been scheduled to meet a few of my brothers through Islam.

It hadn't been hard to spot them sitting at a table in a restaurant filled with Caucasians.

Brother Naheem waved me over to them.

"As-Salam Alaikum," I greeted each of my brothers.

"Wa-Alalikum As Salaam.: They replied.

I sat down, and a waitress took out orders, then we got down to business.

Naheem had been the only one out of the three I actually had a bond with before Islam. Like me, he'd been a prior gang member, but from the other side of the flag, but like me, Allah had come before everything else in his life.

Yamell cleared his throat, then leaned in. "What would make a man crazy enough to shoot up a Mosque?"

"Like us, my past life is crazy. Like me, I'm sure everyone at this table knows somebody who wants them dead." I looked from each set of eyes in search of my answer.

"Anybody who ever came for Amir became the name of a new gang in my city Ahky," Amir said with a lot of aggression in his voice. I'd given him a pass as it only being passion. "Where you from, brother? I hear an East Coast accent," I questioned.

"North Philly, boy."

My left hand slily slid to my waist out of instinct, basically reacting to Amir's aggressive demeanor, then the thought of committing an unforgivable sin caused me to rethink my actions and bring it down a bit.

That's just how them niggas from over there talk.

"Brother Naheem tells me you have a business proposition that can be big with the right pipeline?" Amir's tone had gotten turned all the way down, letting me know how essential I'd been to the plan he's spoken of.

"I'm able to get prescription pills for the low, and with the help of brother Yamell's trucking company and your connects on the east coast, there's a big amount we can all make," I explained.

The waitress had come with our food causing us to pause for the moment.

"I'll just give my people the heads up, and it's all steak and gravy, ahk," Amir said.

After everything had gotten put in place and agreed upon, I made my way out with a million-dollar play, one step away from being put in motion.

Chapter 27
Juice

I thought Freeze being alive and breathing free air really fucked with me, and to be real, it did but waking up without my brotha's chain felt like waking up and dying every day like the white chick in the movie Happy Death Day. I knew the fuck nigga Alphonzo still had it because there wasn't a soul online flexin' with it. The thought of not having it made me wanna kill something, which brought me to the hospital.

It had been a couple of minutes to three in the morning when I stepped through the hospital doors with one agenda. Kill the fuck nigga Twin.

I couldn't believe the bougie nigga Jaxx had the audacity to still serv Twin knowing he'd been drillin' with us which made him an enemy to any sucka who wanted smoke with Murda Gang than to really season the beef Twin had been sellin' the same work Jaxx supplied us with at a lower rate.

I knew exactly where he'd been laid up at because I had Jessie get the details for me, then I posted out front in the parking lot, sitting in my car waiting for all his visitors to leave.

When I got to his door, he'd been sleeping with a blanket over him. The bulge by his stomach area let me know he'd been strapped.

I tip-toed to him, snatched the cover off him, and relieved him of the pistol with the attachments.

"Blood, what the fuck!"

"I ain't take you for the snitch type, so stop the yellin' before it starts." A devilish grin made its way across my face while he laid there mean muggin me.

I back-stepped into the hallway, making sure no one had been out there. Then after seeing the coast had been clear, I stepped back in the room, closed the door then turned the volume up on the T.V. up.

His face said all I needed to know. There'd been no reason to question what I already knew the answer to. I'd been waiting for a reason to put Twin in a Backwood and know I had it.

"O-Dawg gon' have the whole Town chasing down yo set for ten bands because that's all you fuck niggas is worth, blood."

I chucked at his lil going away speech, "Those are the words you leaving us with."

I planned on smothering him with a pillow, but since his glizzy had a silencer with a stick on it, I put it to use.

Pew-Pew!!

I dropped two in his face, wiped his burner clean of my prints, dropped it where I found it, and then took the stairs down to the first floor, where I made my exit.

It seemed like Twin's murder had been a relief to society, at least that' how the news ran it.

Hitman for Crime Organization shot dead in the hospital bed!

The Oregonian had that bitch nigga, Twin, suspected of Olay, Ralo, Fattz, and about six other bodies that were mostly M.G.'s points.

I smirked at the screen after seeing his face followed by the alleged bodies he'd caught then. Every Mob Life member's face appeared on the screen, and a chill feeling rattled my body looking at the last living Mob Life member. The Mob Boss O-Dawg.

I knew after killing Twin I had a lash Jaxx. It pained me to the core that the only person I'd conceded ever in life to be a big homie to me would allow me to starve, knowing what came with the life we'd chosen.

"Yea, I gotta get 'em."

"You gotta get who?" Jessie mumbled with a mouth full of dick.

"Nobody." I put my hand on the back of her head. She swatted my hand away and started sucking the life out of me.

"Slurp, slurp, slurp."

"Oh shit! Fuck!" I gave out a bitch nigga's whimper as my toes curled. I felt my nut building up from my thighs, making my legs shake as she sped up.

Ring, ring, ring.

One of our phones started going off, but neither of us was in the position to find out.

"Ugh!" I shot my unborn down her throat.

"Now, Pappi, wouldn't you want to wake up to that every day?" She looked up at me while licking my remainders off her lips with a smile.

I wasn't ready for anything serious with her, but I didn't know how to break it to her, nor did I care to. I knew her feelings for me were strong, but I had too much real shit going on in my life to give her emotions any thought.

"You might wanna watch this one. He's sneaky." She handed me my phone with a wet wash rag.

I'd seen I had a missed call and a few unread texts from JoJo, so I hit him up after I got fresh.

"What's the triv?"

"Blood the homie got caught in the 'spital!" His tone had been real depressing.

I had to fight hard not to laugh in his face as I thought back to Twin's 'going away speech? I closed my eyes, then took a deep breath, exhaled then told him what he wanted to hear.

"My and Twin had our disagreements, but O-Dawg is my big bro, and you're my lil bro, so whenever you ready, I'm at your disposal."

I fell into full fledge actor's mode on some real Michael B. Jordan shit, and nobody but me knew it.

"A nigga gotta figure a few things out first, bro… but I do need to holla at you some serious shit blood. But not like this, so I can come to where you at?"

The seriousness in his tone low-key concerned me, but I didn't want to pry.

"Drop the addy and give me 'bout an hour at the most, lil bro."

"Yup."

I knew no one who mattered had seen me go in or out of the hospital the night I got Twin outside of Jessie nobody else knew I'd pulled that skit, so I felt safe in that department.

"Where you going?" Jessie asked, fresh out of the shower, still dripping wet while brushing her hair.

"I'll be right back. I just gotta handle some shit."

"Not before I get some dick." She started unloosening my belt, and I let my lil head take over.

Chapter 28
Juice

"You think he know 'bout you and Jessie?" Gunna asked as we pulled up JoJo's apartment complex.

I'd just given him the condensed version of me and Jessie along with what went down at my mom's spot and the shit with Twin.

"I ain't a hunnid about it, but I do think some suspicion crossed him." I broke down the gas station incident where JoJo had pulled up and found me and Jessie arguing.

I needed a real nigga' advice and the only person I knew who'd be all the way real with me and tell what I needed to hear was my twin demon Gunna.

He cut the car off and looked me dead in the eyes. "Bro, don't sleep on that lil nigga or any of his niggas. Yo love for a nigga almost got you taken away from the people that love you."

My daughters' faces had flashed in my head the second he'd finished his sentence because there hadn't been a soul living who knew how close I'd been to dying by the hands of a person I considered my lil brother like my nigga Gunna.

Gunna had been the one who stepped in Naughty's funeral with me, no one else, just us and our smacks, so he knew firsthand how dangerous JoJo could get.

I genuinely smiled, something I hadn't given in some time, and said, "You never tell a nigga what he wanna hear."

"If I did, I'd only be a self-proclaimed real nigga."

We tucked our heats, then walked into lil bro's spot, gave the regular daps, and got down to business.

Ghost's energy had been a lil standoffish, leading me to believe the smoke hadn't fully cleared. Black had seemed a lil too excited to see Gunna for my taste.

It wouldn't surprise me to find out he's gay.

"Them Rose City Crabs did that," Ghost expressed his belief in a low killa's tone.

"Them nigga ain't with the smoke. They are drug-free, blood. Crabs don't want it blood." Gunna just to make it some Blood and Crip shit.

To be real, I felt bro played his part to the fullest, especially after knowing what I'd just told him, which left me with no choice but to fall in character.

"Bro, why you think it's them?" I couldn't sit quietly that would have given me away:

"Bro, you don't remember the shootout I told you we were in when Twin got hit?" JoJo asked.

I shook my head.

"Caught niggas lackin in the Vill bounced out and got activated. Ghost smoked Nutcase, and Lil Nuts caught a few shells, but he survived. Ghost had realized then you ain't kill sis??

I noticed Gunna's hand shift to his waist as he gave me a quick glance. I shook my head, letting him know to fall back. We were out gunned, plus I felt the Drama Gang niggas could be useful in helping to clear the beef on our plate.

I raced Ghost then asked the billion-dollar question, "What made you believe I ain't do it?"

The room got real quiet for a few seconds.

"Before the pussy got off, he yelled tell Juice his brotha next."

He didn't even have to name-drop. I knew he'd been talking about the fuck nigga Alphonzo faggot ass Harris. It seemed like God wanted the fuck nigga to live every time I had him dead to rights. He kept escaping my grip.

"No one in this room got a line on him?"

Silence came after my question, getting me a lil hot.

"We gon' really have to buckle down and do some real home-work, blood," Gunna stated the obvious.

I needed to kill Freeze so bad that I'd been on the verge of walking in the Mosque barefaced burner in hand and smoking that bitch, then offering the same treatment for anyone who felt a way about it. Drugs, sex, or even being with my kids couldn't cure the feeling of needing a fuck nigga dead. Senseless bodies were piling up, making the streets hot, and to top it off, I didn't have any work to push.

Meditating, praying, or yoga had never been my way of stress-relieving, but I needed something bad to help me cope although I didn't feel worthy of it, I had to take my final resort.

Marcellus Allen

Chapter 29
Juice

The rain had fizzled out, but the wind had a strong blow causing my eyes to water a bit as I bounced out the Bentley woozy off a duce of syrup. Stumbling to the realist nigga to ever walk the planet's tombstone.

I took a few minutes to stare at his tombstone before speaking. "Bro, you don't know how much I miss you. How much yo lil bro needs you." I paused, allowing tears to fall.

Normally, I would have fought back the tears, but I'd been bottling in so much for so long I just let it all fall.

"I got no help with this shit out here. You left me out here all alone. You got nieces who will never meet their dad's idol," I wiped my tears with the back of my hand.

"I know you feel like I failed you because I'm here without yo chain. Freeze got it, and he's still breathing." More tears fell as I took a deep breath, then angrily slapped my chest and yelled, "I feel like I failed me, but I ain't a failure, bro. On you and Omar's grave, that bitch nigga Alphonzo will not breathe a breath of spring air. Bro, I love you and send Omar's fat ass my love."

I laughed a lil just thinking about my nigga Omar running around with his shirt off and chains on like Rick Ross or something.

"On Murda Gang, I'm sending y'all some suckas to beat on," I vowed, then walked to my car feeling a lot less anxious.

For the past few days, I'd been chilling with my bitch in the crib, getting a piece of mind. It's crazy how much Breonna's so much of an opposite person from the bitches that I'm used to dealing with. She never complained about my whereabouts or other bitches. She'd been content with spending time with a real nigga whenever she got it.

I sat at the foot of the bed, phone in hand, scrolling niggas' pages and laughing at certain R.I.P. posts while Bre cooked.

O-Dawg had made a long post about Twin's death. I started to Tweet out L.O.L. after R.I.P. Twin, but I needed O-Dawg for the play I'd been setting.

"This bitch is obsessed." I fumed after sending Jessie to voicemail for the third time straight.

Jessie's annoyed me to the point that whenever I wasn't fuckin' her, I wished I never fucked her. But she had a W.A.P. for real, and her head game's in its own lane.

"Daddy, who got you in here trippin'? Bre walked in carrying my food.

"Nobody important." I sat my phone down and started digging in my food.

"If it's a bad bitch, I don't see why we both can't have her?" I looked up with a raised eyebrow.

Bre should have been my bitch.

Chapter 30
Juice

"No Bueno. I'm not that type of bitch." Jessie declined her only real chance to be with a real nigga.

"I figured since you were always blowing me up, I can present a compromise so everybody can eat, B." I stood in her living room, testing her to see how far I could go.

She stood with one hand on her hip while pointing at me with the other one and cussin me out in Spanish, looking sexy as fuck, even though I didn't understand a word she'd said.

I just stood there adding fuel to the fire looking at her with a sideways smirk.

"So, what's the verdict on that? I gotta lil baddy down with whole shit on the gang." I tossed my pitch again.

Her fist balled as her face scrunched up, "Ugh! Ah! If I didn't respect your gansta, Pappi." She shook her head. "You just don't know."

"Have you ever tried it, though?"

"Bye, Juice. I gotta get ready for work." She stormed into the room and got dressed.

I didn't want to, but after she confirmed she didn't wanna share a real nigga, I had to let lil bro know the triv. I didn't want to restart our relationship on some foul type of shit, and I could never forget O-Dawg explaining to my whole gang how his sneaky acts broke up the Mob.

Lil bro had been at Woodlawn Park with a couple of Hit Squad nigga that I really didn't give one fuck about. But just in case shit did get a lil weird, I had two niggas with me who had no problem making a mess. Mask and Gunna.

"Big bro, what was so urgent?" JoJo asked as we dapped.

"I gotta let you know some serious shit," I replied, looking at Jimmy, who'd been with a few other niggas that I didn't care to meet.

Tension had been in the air, at least that's how I'd felt, or it could have just been my guilty conscience for killing Marcell. Either way, I had to do a low-key temp-check.

"Jimmy, what's up?" I cracked the ice.

"Sup Juice," Jimmy replied, sounding like he'd forced while giving me one of those 'Let me get this nigga out my face daps.'

Should have felt like that when my brother died, weak ass Blood niggas.

I brushed that shit off and holla'd at lil bro while Mask and Gunna holla'd at Jimmy and his homies.

When we got out of ear range of the crowd, I kept it solid with lil bro.

"I have been fuckin' Jessie, gang."

He stood stiff for a few seconds. I took it as him, letting it all soak in while we stared each other down without blinking once.

"You couldn't tell me that over the phone?"

"Naw, gang. I had to look you in the eyes and be honest with you."

I explained how O-Dawg wished he would have brought the shit and Jersey Joe to Burnside before taking it upon himself to kill Jersey Joe and how it broke up the Mob.

"I'm 'posed to be mad 'cause she 'let' you smash? Keisha had moved on with crab nigga, and at the end of the day, you're my bro. I would be hot at you even if you were with sis and didn't hit Jessie. She too bad for any real nigga to pass up. Do she be talking in Spanish when you be hittin?"

I smiled while nodding hella fast. "With the accent and all, on the gang." I threw it up.

His eyes had lit up after I explained how fire her head game is. *Ding!*

My phone started dancing in my pocket. I pulled it out and saw it had been Jessie. I started not to check, but the pic had been of a couple opps in the club she worked at. I showed lil bro the footage.

"Blood, that's them lil Rose City niggas. I went to school with them soft ass nigga," JoJo informed while studying the screen.

The second he handed me back my phone, another pic came in showing the fuck nigga Shotta having the time of his life with a couple of new niggas.

"That club should be called oceans with all the crabs in there." Lil bro stated.

"Well, the shark is coming to eat blood," Gunna added.

I knew the word crab would snatch Gunna's attention but not while he'd been having a whole 'nother convo with Jimmy. But then again, it's Gunna, a nigga who lived for smoking shit.

I sent Jessie a text. *Keep 'em there*

A weird feeling touched the pit of my stomach, making me feel very uneasy. For a split second, it felt like the world stopped.

"What's pop'n ahk?" Some deep-voiced nigga banged. My hand swung to my waist, but the party had already started.

Boca! Boca! Boca! Boca! Boca! Boca!

Everybody scattered in hopes of living the park alive. I ran, hid behind a tree for a second, then returned the gift.

"Murda Gang," I banged while knockin' at the black Navigator.

Bloaw! Boca! Boca! Blaow! Bloaow! Boca Boca!

Me, lil bro, Gunna, and Mask were trying to flip that truck while the Hit-Squad niggas did the same shit they did when my brotha died. Nothing.

"Nigga, who fuck was that?" Mask growled as the truck smashed up the block.

I shrugged my shoulders, "Some nigga who just brought a one way to hell."

Me and Gunna looked at each other then that's when it hit me. *Had to be them niggas from the Mosque.*

"Everybody strap up! We going on a field trip," Jimmy directed, then led his young boys to his car.

"Look down the street," I pointed out.

"This shit must be personal," JoJo said as we saw the Navi bending the corner on the double back.

As the truck came roaring out direction, I threw shots at that bitch tryin' to get it to swerve, wreck or do something, but the bullets did nothing, and it kept coming.

"That mafucka is bulletproof," I mumbled, then turned around warned my niggas. "That bitch is bulletproof. We gotta get up outta here."

Boca! Boca! Boca! Bloaw! Bloaw! Boca!

Shots rang out from both sides, causing me to do what I felt was best for my future. Hid.

Shit!

The Navi scratched off. The shots stopped but were quickly replaced by sirens.

Chapter 31
Juice

"You think we can get in with the smacks?" JoJo asked from the backseat.

We were sitting in the club's parking lot four deep, putting our play together. I switched rides and hopped in Gunna's shit, which didn't take too much time. No more than twenty minutes later, we were on a mission.

"We gon' just wait for them niggas to come out and do 'em dirty for Twin blood." Gunna threw the set up, looking real believable.

"For Twin, we gon' closed they casket lil bro," I fronted with Oscar-worthy passion in my voice.

In the rearview mirror, I saw Mask shaking his head, and I knew he'd been questioning why I would care to ride for a nigga I never cared for.

The only person in the car that knew I'd been responsible for Twin's deaths had been Gunna, and I planned to keep it that way, at least for the time being.

"Look." Gunna pointed out our prey.

I cracked a smile seeing the lumps and bruises on Shotta's face while he stepped out with a chick on each side.

Ding!

They're leaving right now. Jessie's text read.

"That's them bitch nigga, right there," I growled while feeling my anger rise, looking at two of the niggas who were in that video cheering Lazy on while he C-Walked with my brotha's chain on.

"Frog and Do-Wrong," JoJo name-dropped the cheerleaders who'd been rocking white tees that said 'Nutup' in blue.

"I wanna see Frog hop away from these shells," Mask joked while we watched Frog and Do-Wrong stop to chop it up with Shotta.

Blood dripped from our fangs, ready to bite down on something.

"Naw, me and big bro got them," JoJo called dibs on the Rose City Crips.

The second Frog and Da-Wrong started walking away from Shotta, we pulled our ski masks down and slid out.

Me and lil bro crept through the real low cutting behind parked cars with one thing on our minds. Adding to the scoreboard.

"We need to stop and get something to eat first." My head swung in the direction the voice had come from. I tapped lil bro and pointed where I'd heard the chick's voice.

"Cuz that not an issue," a nigga said in a high-pitched voice.

Boca! Boca! Boca! Boca!

Gunna and Mask got it poppin early.

"Cuz somebody shooting! Get the strap."

"Ahhh!" a bitch screamed after Frog pushed her in front of him. Me and JoJo ran towards Frog and Do-Wrong.

"Lazy up there waiting for you." JoJo taunted.

Boca! Boca! Bloaw! Bloaw!

"Aw, man! Frog can't hop no more?" JoJo joked after hitting Frog.

I ran past the bitch trailing Do-Wrong all the way to his car. I'd been a few feet away, but when I saw the driver's door open, and he reached for something, I sprinted to him fast.

"Don't even think about it, pussy. You did all that hooting hollerin' for the dead locs now you 'bout to become a dead loc!'"

"That was free-"

Boca! Boca! Boca!

"Tell it to somebody that cares." I lifted the gold rope with the Rose City pendant hanging from it and left him in his car with his ass in the air and his face down.

I headed to the car and stopped after finding JoJo standing over Frog, dumping shell after shell in him, going in overkill. He'd been so deep in the zone when I tapped him, he turned around and upped on me.

"Hol' up brodie, it's me." I took a few steps back.

"My bad blood." He put his shit away.

Holes were leaking blood all over Frog's face. I stared at the lifeless pussy for a few seconds, just taking it all in, then I remembered what we'd even come to the club for in the first place.

"For my nigga, Twin," I capped, then dropped my last three shells in Frog.

Skirrt!

"We gotta shake!" Gunna pulled up and yelled.

We hopped and did just that.

Marcellus Allen

Chapter 32
Juice

The butterflies in my stomach must have been fighting something serious, and to make things crazier, I felt over-anxious like a nigga on a home invasion with every second that passed leading up to the biggest decision I've ever made since catching my first body. I took a deep breath then exhaled as the basic, but clean Oldsmobile slowed down.

"Sup." I tried killing my anxiety by acknowledging the driver as I hopped in.

He just nodded at me.

The whole drive had been quiet like we were trying to read each other.

The silence broke when we got to his basement.

"I got half mill for whoever brings me the nigga who killed my lil bro." His eye stared into mine, and for the first time since meeting the bougie nigga, I saw a killa lurking.

"Soon as I heard about it, I had to put a soul in the ground." I gave a portion of the truth.

"Is that right?" he questioned my word as if I'd been cap'n or some shit.

"Yea, that's right. We had our lil disagreement, but we don' drilled shit together." I defended my word with a reminder.

The tone in his voice had told me all that he needed me to know. Twin out the way, but I'd come too far to turn around. I wanted to give him a chance to fix it because he's the reason I pushed a Bentley, but all that stopped when his personal phone rang.

"Is this shit a joke?" he questioned while staring at the screen and smiling like he'd been on an M.T.V. prank show.

"Naw, it ain't." I upped on him.

"Put that shit away. That ain't even your style." He answered the call then turned his back to me as if he could just talk his problems out.

I grabbed a handful of his fat, nasty, Rasta-looking dreads and stuck the cold steel against his temple.

119

"We got yo family. Now we want the money and all the dope. It's your life or theirs. Pick nigga."

"Pick nigga," he mocked me. "Why you gotta be so aggressive? You already got a gun to my head, and my family's being held captive. You wanna nigga to cry or give one of them humanitarian speeches? You one of them niggas who need to do stupid shit to prove you still down, huh? The way-"

Smack!

"Shut the fuck up! I need to think," I spat after smacking him with my heat a few times.

He let out a couple of ow's and aw's from the floor while I'd been laying the smackdown, but throughout the whole beat down, he was smiling.

Smack, smack!!

"How it feels to cross the nigga that made you?"

I got down one knee and just beat the life out of his eye.

"You feel like a man?" His face and shirt were covered in his own blood, and he still found time to crack a joke.

His lil commentary irked the fuck out of me to the point I'd been ready to just smoke the funny nigga and leave with my shipment, but I had too many people who depended on me. Plus, when O-Dawg decided to put that bag on me, I wanna be so far out of reach but in his face at the same time.

"Outta breath already, lil buddy? Must be the drugs no wonder yo be needing a re-up so fast-"

"Nigga, you just begging to die."

"I have been to Paris, China, and even Africa. I blew mills on jewelry drove the best cars. I mean, I lived. I mean, really lived. I don't care to die. Just spare my wife and daughters."

Hearing the word daughters made me think about Lisa and Ashley. I would definitely give my life for theirs without hesitation, so we agreed if he led us to all the guap and dope, I'd spare his family.

We hopped on the Facetime with TJ and Gunna and watched them move a living room couch to the side, then move a piece of carpet that covered a box-shaped hole that had been filled with a small digital safe. After getting the passcode and seeing it stuffed with blue stripes, I knew something had been off.

"You been getting money for a long time. Where the rest at?" I stood over him, smack aimed at his face and his phone in the other.

He led us to two more safes the size of the digital one and then a big one tucked in the master room with at least a quarter mill of small face hundreds and twenties plus fifty bricks. Finally, he asked the big question.

"How you find out where my fam stayed?"

"Waited for yo mom to visit O-Dawg. That took a month. I followed her home and waited for you to pull up. That took a few weeks. Found out who yo wife was, and Facebook did the rest."

He started clappin' as if I'd won a Grammy. "Just think if you invested that much time in yo grind, where'd you be?'

"I didn't want to, but you pulled my plate off the table, so," I kneeled down and whispered, "I killed Twin."

He tried reaching for my gun like a real braveheart after hearing I smoked Twin, but I just backed away. Plus, he'd been too weak.

Boca! Boca! Boca! Boca!

Blood splashed on my face, shirt, jeans, and shoes. I used my shirt to wipe my face while I looked down at the soulless body of the person who'd provided me with the tools to get rich. Out of nowhere, a disappointing feeling came over me. I chalked it up as remorse far crossing O-Dawg. He and Jaxx were the only two niggas that wanted to see me shine.

"I gotta get outta here." I searched the house and found another seventy bands, two Draco's, a pound of runts, and a couple of bricks off soft.

Marcellus Allen

Chapter 33
Freeze

It seemed like the Lil Juice nigga lost all hope in getting his brotha's chain back and settled for knocking down a few of my lil homies in training. Honestly, I didn't give two fucks about them niggas. They were just peons set to protect the king. What I did care about was my money, and lately, I've been getting a lot of it.

Me and my wife's real estate company had been flourishing to a degree only Allah could bring man. Aaliyah's been doing so good in school it should be a crime. Business with my Muslim brothers had been flowing smoothly, so I guess everything's on the upside.

My black Escalade truck circled the block for any treacherous backdoor activities and to make sure I wasn't being followed. I spotted Trey coming out of the spot we'd been set to meet at. Even though the spot's him, I parked a few houses down just to blend in with the black.

"What's crackin' cuz?" He dapped me with our hood-shake.

"Cuz, I'm out here tryin' to get to it." My eyes scanned our surroundings, something the streets taught me early, but jail taught me to analyze individuals, and so far, Trey seemed regular.

"We gotta get some shit straight, cuz." He led the way.

The moment we'd gotten inside, he updated me on how the homies were doing.

"Cash and Forty got snatched for a body." He walked to the kitchen and came back with a few bottles of prescription pills.

"A body? This seems random, loco."

To be real, I'd been so confused I had to take a seat on the couch to put things in some type of perspective. I hadn't been watching the news or any T.V. because I'd spent a bulk of time in jail watching T.V., plus social media had never been my scene. All of the snitching and Police attention people craved on their social sites weren't a place to be putting your business on unless you wanted to get put in jail.

"Oh, shit, I forgot." He sat the pill bottles on the table in front of me, slid to one of the bedrooms, and came back with a backpack for me.

"That ain't even the kicker. They are down for my baby momma's body. I went to get my son from his grandma's spot in Salem, and he told me it was two of his uncles." He put air quotes on the word uncles. "He told me and the cops he caught his mom doing nasty stuff with in the past."

"I thought Lil Juice sent them pictures, though," I stated, putting the pill bottles in the backpack.

"He did. But the only thing that makes any sense is they got pointed out because my son remembers them coming through and fucking her."

Even though he wasn't committed to that baby momma outside of co-parenting, it doesn't give someone in our immediate circle reason to smash. Baby moms are off-limits to anyone perceived as our brotha.

"That's disrespecting a niggas crip'n for real."

"Shit crazy," he agreed, then shrugged his shoulders.

"It is what it is. But on another note, with them niggas out the way for the moment, plus Do-Wrong and Frog dead, I got more weight than I can handle. The plug ain't let a nigga decrease the shipment."

This couldn't have come at a better time.

"I might have a way to move that shit fast!" I gave him a quick rundown on the shit I'd been doing with Amis, Yamell, and Naheem.

"That sounds good. Plus, my plants in the back a be fully budded real soon.

The spot we were in had been a grow house strictly for growing bomb ass weed and doing small business transactions.

We talked a lil while longer about our business plans then I got out of there.

Chapter 34
Freeze

"Another A what I tell you? Put in the work, and Allah will take care of the rest." I congratulated my daughter for scoring an A on her math test.

"I wasn't as challenging as before. You know why?"

"You studied." I pinched her cheek, playing with her.

"Because you're home, daddy, and it makes me more relaxed knowing my dad's here."

Man, that melted my heart to the point I started resenting myself for spending two weeks away from her just to find some lil knucklehead lost and confused brotha. I wished I'd been able to sit and have a man to man with Lil Juice and allow him to see that Allah has more in store for us than taking the lives of our own kind. I wished he'd been able to forgive me for my past life and respect that I'm not living like that anymore, but too much has happened, and here we are.

"Lonzo. Brother Trey's here!" Fatimah yelled.

"I'll be down in a second," I turned to Aaliyah. "I do owe you something, right?"

She nodded with an ear-to-ear smile.

I pulled a knot from my pocket and slid her two-hundred-dollar bills, then whispered, "Don't tell mommy. The extra hundreds for motivation."

"I got an A in science, and I always keep an A in P.E."

A hustler just like her daddy. Some wouldn't call it wise to give an eleven-year-old four hundred dollars cash,,,,,, but a person can't learn to stack without anything to save, and I wanted my baby girl to learn that early.

I got downstairs and found Trey talking to my wife dressed in a long Islamic shirt that cut off near the knees and a pair of nut huggin jeans with rips all over them that had his Crip'n looking gay. I had to really look at cuz because the real locs didn't care for all that swag shit before I felt it was Gangland for real.

I let my presence be known with a loud cough. Me and Trey greeted like Muslims do.

"Brother Trey was just telling me about his wife Lakeisha, who sells Islamic products through Q.V.C. with the *Shark Tank* lady, and she has a podcast."

He held his chin up then spoke in some deep sports announcer's voice, "Living is teaching. You guys should stop by sometime. Three nights a week, we have local rappers, athletes, politicians, and everyday people like us."

I wasn't moved by it one bit, nor did I care to find out what the fuck a podcast was. However, for the sake of my beautiful wife's interest, I put on a smile.

"Maybe later something," I replied.

Fatimah must have gotten the message because she went upstairs without saying another word.

As soon as she left upstairs, Trey started to speak but stopped him because I didn't hear the door shut.

"Let me get a minute." I quietly walked up a couple of stairs, where I found Fatimah eavesdropping.

"I'm a step out for a few minutes, babe."

She flashed a smile then nodded.

Chapter 35
Juice

Since hittin Jaxx for the bricks and bread, life had been on the up. The only thing that's been troubling me is knowing that bitch nigga Freeze is still with the chain I swore to protect with my life, but I hoped to bring him or one of his pussy homies out from hiding with all the stunting and shit I'd been doing online with Do-Wrong's chain on.

"This bitch lit blood," Gunna stated.

He wasn't lying either. There'd been bad bitches from all over in the spot tryin' to get in a real nigga's section and flick up. Normally I wouldn't be caught doing shit in Salem but going to visit a homie in jail or some type of business, but Mask had insisted we go out and live a lil.

"Are you guys' rappers or something?" Some bad lil white chick asked.

"Yea, we're body wrappers." I dapped Gunna while we shared a laugh.

"It's just I've never seen you guys in Salem before."

That's because we some real rich Northeast niggas," Masked hopped in the mix.

I signaled for the bouncer to let her through then I introduced myself.

"Juice," I put my hand.

"Victoria. I'm sorry, but I'm a hugger." She stepped forward with both arms opened, forcing me into a hug.

"Are you guys doing shots or something?"

"Shots," I let out a light laugh, "Naw baby, real niggas do bottles. Want one?"

"I'm not going to be able to drink it all."

"I don't care if you pour it on somebody. But always remember when you're in a real nigga's section, all you gotta do is look the part and listen."

"That's right, girl," the dark skin chick Gunna had been holla'n at did my ab-libs.

I signaled for the waitress to bring another bottle so we could turn up to the max.

"We want all the smoke." Everybody in our section yelled out the hook to Future and Young Thug's song, *We Want All The Smoke.*

It seemed like the whole club had been in our section. I put my bottle in the air and two-stepped with Victoria's fine ass.

Normally, I wouldn't even be entertaining a white broad, but baby reminded me of a thick-ass Megan Fox, leaving a young killa no choice but to pursue the kill.

"You're really tall." She complimented me while looking up at me.

I took a swig off my Ace of Spades bottle, "What are you doing after this?"

Being a rich real nigga made me think differently. All that tryin' to finesse my way into bitch's panties died the night we got Jaxx.

She shrugged her shoulders, set the bottle down, kneeled down, looked up at me, and said, "Pour it in my mouth."

Gunna hopped off the couch, being extra as always, and yelled out, "Certified head giver blood."

I slowly poured the drink in her mouth, and then she used her tongue to wipe clean whatever had hit the side of her mouth.

I watched her rise up slow with a hand between my legs, making my meat damn near tear a hole through my jeans as her fingers traced my dick print.

"I think I can take it all." She squeezed my meat, then turned around and started bussin' it wide to the City Girls and Cardi B's joint *Twerk.*

"That nigga looks familiar, gang." Mask pointed at some older cat draped in designer with jewelry on at the bar with three baddies.

"Blood that's the soft nigga, D-Roc. I wouldn't pay him no mind," Gunna suggested.

Bro did have a point but catching a sucka rolling dolo could really bring the hoe out of a nigga.

"Bro, I'm 'bout to pull this nigga's card," I got Mask's attention. "Go live." I turned to Victoria. "Can you excuse me for a second?" I didn't even give the bitch time to answer. I just made my way to D-Roc and pushed up with the full-court press.

"What's pop'n gang? You D-Roc?" I pressed.

He turned around, and that's when Gunna and I stepped up side by side, closing in all the space. We didn't even leave him space to breathe.

I could see he tried running my face through his memory date, seeing if I registered or not, but I ain't the waiting type nigga, so I asked the question I knew he'd been thinking.

"Yea, I'm Murda Gang Juice," I through the set up. "I heard niggas trippin' and speaking on my gang."

He took a few steps back, bumping into a bar stool, causing Gunna to chuckle.

He caught his balance the surrendered with both hands in the air," Look, fam, whatever happened with y'all and my lil homies, that's on y'all. I'm getting money, period, and that's all niggas know D-Roc for."

He tried pushing past me tryin' a get to them bitches who left him for dead, but I stopped him.

"I started Flip Gang and Pusha World. What you gon' do about it?"

"All that rah-rah shit is for the young boys, man." He copped his plea then he pushed past us without even grabbing the drinks he paid for.

"I should cook that nigga right here in Salem," Gunna growled.

For a real Northeast nigga to get cooked in Salem would be such a devastating blow to a real nigga's legacy. The thought alone made we wanna get back to the Town asap.

Chapter 36
Juice

"Lil bro, what's the triv?" I dapped JoJo as I stepped in his spot then did the same to Ghost and Black.

"Trippin' off you movin' 'round this bitch like you rockin' the Ironman suit or some shit." JoJo joked, cracking Black up but barely getting a smile out of Ghost.

It took a minute for me to get it, but after I heard my voice coming from the T.V., my palm slapped my forehead as it all came back to me.

They were watching the video on how I did D-Roc the last night at the club. It had been uploaded from the phone to the T.V.

"Big bro, you pulled every ounce of hoe out the nigga blood." JoJo gave me my props.

"Now had that been the Ghost nigga. Ghost would have slapped that nigga right in front of his bitches and made him crawl out the club like crabs." Ghost had it on too thick.

"Why is this nigga constantly repeating his own name like he tryin' to remember a phone number?" Black-faced Ghost, "Blood, I'm worried about you. And Juice, you're the one who fucked him up with all that Dark Lo."

"Dark Lo be talking that shit."

"Facts." Ghost added, giving a slow *Godfather* mob boss head nod.

While JoJo went to get my guap, I looked at how I did D-Roc, and from the outside looking in, I'd been able to see how weak and deflated his energy had gotten.

"That's a buck fifty right there, big bro. In a minute, I'ma be coppin' with you, not from you." He handed me the black duffle bag.

It sounded like he'd been playing, but all good jokes contain truth, and he asked about my plug lil too many times for my comfort. I never liked puzzles as a kid, and I damn sho' ain't fuckin' with them as an adult. I never liked being confused because anything that confuses me must be untangled. Rather than letting the emotional side of a real nigga show, I let it roll off my back and played it easy.

"A lil more work, bro, and you gon' be there." I left on that note.

With Twin out the way, work's been moving fast, but the shit that interested me the most had been the fact I didn't get one call from O-Dawg. I looked that nigga up and saw that he'd been moved out to Eastern Oregon to some city where I knew Blacks were to them. Suspicion ate at my conscious, so I had Bre send my nigga some flicks and a few Straight stuntin' magazines to help him with his time since I did just make it a lot harder.

Britt had invited me over for dinner, which seemed a lil odd because she'd been trippin' hard about that shit that happened with Flip, but how could I blame her knowing our daughter's life could have gotten taken just as easy as I took Flip's life.

She changed the locks on me after I lost control and smacked, so I had to wait at the door like a trick or treater.

The door opened, and the sight of seeing her really fucked me up.

She had her hair wrapped in a bun with the baby hairs greased down like that rapper chick Saweetie. The blue coochie-cutting jean short she wore had her ass looking real fluffy.

"Here." I handed her a bouquet of roses.

"Thank you…but you didn't have to. We're just having a family dinner."

"Yea, but I wanted to. Are you gonna invite me in?"

"Daddy, daddy!" Ashley screamed the second she stepped out of the bathroom and ran to me.

"Hey, baby girl." I scooped her up and started planting kisses all over her forehead and cheeks.

"Daddy, are you staying for dinner? And did you bring mommy a gift and not me?" Because that's not right." She turned my face by the chin and made a mad face.

She had me and Britt cracking up. I couldn't believe how mature and smart my youngest baby girl had gotten.

I shrugged my shoulders," I don't know; I gotta check my pockets. Close yo eyes."

I dug in my pocket, pulled out a jewelry box. I pulled out a small gold rope with a pendant that said Ashley covered in diamonds and placed it around her neck. I could feel Britt's eyes burning a hole through me with every second it took to place it around Ashley's neck.

"Davontae, did you just spend all that money on that girl?" Britt whined with a hint of jealousy in her tone.

"Look in the flowers," I instructed.

"Mom, stop hate'n."

"Yea, mom, stop hate'n," I repeated what Ashley just said while waiting for Britt to open her gift.

She held the chain up. "It says Juice."

Niggas gotta know who they are competing with." I walked on her and wrapped my arms around her waist.

She created distance with a stiff arm like a running back, denying me access to the goods, "Too soon, it's only dinner. But can you put this on me, please?"

The cold shoulder had me feeling like a straight weeny for dropping ten on a necklace for a bitch I couldn't even smash. I nursed my bruised ego by reminding myself I put 'us' in the place we're in.

She did say too soon.

She placed a finger over her lips and pointed at Ashley.

My baby had gone from pointing at an invisible camera person to holding her chain up and rappin'.

"Cash me outside, Cash me outside." Ashley rapped.

"Baby girl who you want to catch you outside?"

"No, daddy, it's the Bhad Baby song."

"Cash me outside." Britt corrected.

My face gave me away. I didn't know shit they were talking about, so Britt grabbed her phone and showed me a video of some lil girl on *Dr. Phil* acting out and trippin' hard, then another one with the lil girl in a video with Kodak Black.

While Britt cooked, Ashley and I made Tik-Toc videos, doing lil funny dances, just having father and daughter fun.

Chapter 37
Juice

I just knew after putting that bling on Britt's neck, I'd capped my night off with some deserved good pussy, but had I said that's how I capped my night off, it would be cap. She sent a real nigga to the couch, and the only reason I'd stayed over was because I promised my baby girl that I'd be there when she woke up.

Two days had passed our family dinner, and business had been going up. Gunna and Mask had taken a trip out to Seattle, where Gunna's people stayed so they could set up shop out there because the streets of Portland were one body away from being conquered by Murda Gang.

Every day I had to remind myself that victory takes time but what really fucked with me was knowing that nigga who killed my bitch and my unborn seed is the same bitch boy who killed my brother and not only has his custom piece, the fuck nigga's still breathing. Just the thought alone made me wanna kill something.

"Let me help you, Pappi." Jessie assisted me with my chains, making sure they didn't get tangled.

I stood in her room staring at myself in her full body-length mirror. I had on three gold ropes, each with a memorial piece for my brotha, Omar, and Naughty hanging off it flooded in ice.

That you, Mami." I didn't care that she saw me rockin' a piece reppin' for my bitch.

She knew firsthand how I felt about Naughty as did any other female in my life, and not a soul living could change that.

I tensed up a bit when Jessie's fingertips touched the piece with Naughty's picture on it. I stood stiff, hoping she wouldn't say something that would cause me to lose it.

"I miss her every day," she said in a low whisper.

I looked down at the scandalous bitch and almost let my anger get the best of me, but I had to remind myself she does serve a purpose.

I got work stashed here nobody knows about.

"Yeah, me too." I went to hug her, but she pushed me away and ran to the bathroom.

I stepped in the hallway and saw her curled over the toilet and ran to her aid, and held her hair back while she threw-up.

Bitch pregnant!

I watched her clear her stomach, and to my surprise, I wasn't even mad, but I wasn't going to say shit until she brought it up.

Just as she went to brush her teeth, my phone rang.

Flash The screen read.

I hit talk and slapped that bitch against my ear. "What's triv gang?"

"Found her. We need to link A.S.A.P."

He couldn't have called at a better time. Just as my anger began to rise thinking about the fuck boy Alphonzo, my nigga hits me with the line on a snitch bitch who wanted to help the pigs bury my nigga alive. Kim.

"Drop the addy gang." I ended the call and waited for his text.

"Pappi, I thought you wanted to spend the day with me since I'm not working." She came in the room after freshin' up.

Her lil possessive ways were starting to work my nerves. I'd never seen it before because the bitch never had a nigga around. A couple of sympathy fucks and we Jay-z and Beyonce.

I closed my eyes, inhaled deep then exhaled slowly to calm myself down before I choked her to death.

"I need yo car."

"Of course, Pappi."

I grabbed the keys to her Hyundai Genesis and got lost somewhere. I don't know why, but lately, my events have been bringing me to the state's capital a lot more than any real Northeast nigga would like to. The car ride had been quiet outside of the King Von songs that played at a respectable volume setting the mood as the soundtrack for the movie we were on our way to make.

"Bitch been tucked off at her aunt's house in some apartments by the railroad tracks," Flash informed with real heat on his words.

Yea, by the downtown section," I hopped off the freeway land-ing downtown Salem then drove to the complex Flash said the bitch had been hiding.

I circled the block looking for anything smirkish, and any es-cape routes in case shit got out of hand.

Had I not known Salem, I would have thought we were in somebody's hood. There weren't any lights on the block we pushed through. Behind the apartments, there'd been an alley.

"It's the second one downstairs all the way in the back."

After being satisfied with our surroundings, I parked and asked a question I normally would have asked prior to a mission.

"Who gave you the assist?"

He avoided my question on some real hoe shit, but before I could press him, we saw Kim in the window.

Marcellus Allen

Chapter 38
Freeze

Trey had hit me with some of the best news I heard since leaving jail. He explained to me that Lil Juice shouldn't make it past the morning on some slimy backdoor shit, plus he had the package I'd been waiting to drop on Amir. Normally I wouldn't answer any calls past nine, but Trey's the only person in the world who can hit me at any time outside of my wife and daughter.

I slid out the bed, being extra quiet trying not to wake Fatimah up. I threw on a sweatsuit, then crept to Aaliyah's room and slowly opened the door, and peeked in. A smile made its way across my face while watching my young queen sleep so peacefully, resembling her mother. I quietly closed her door and made my way to my car.

Twenty minutes later, give or take a few, I pulled up to the location we did business at, but I bent the corner a few times. Since it had been a little after midnight, I didn't have a problem parking in his driveway. As I got to the spot, it hit me.

"Fuck Cuz!" I fumed, realizing I had left my phone at home as I backed into the driveway.

I opened the glove compartment to get my strap and smirked at the sight of that weak ass chain Lil Juice had been holding dear to his heart like it's a Deathrow chain or something. I grabbed it then held it up.

"Yeah, cuz, you got a lil shine on you." I threw it on, grabbed my strap, and slid out.

A somber feeling came over me as I approached the house. A gut feeling told me to turn around after noticing the door cracked, but by then, it had been too late.

Marcellus Allen

Chapter 39
Juice

A gut feeling had told me something had been off, but I just chalked it up as pregame jitters and followed through with the mission.

We pulled our ski masks down and crept the alley entering the apartments from the back.

I heard a couple of weird sounds that caused me to stop and tap brodie.

I whispered, "Hol' up, gang. You hear that?"

He looked at me and dismissed what I said with a hand jester, "I didn't wanna let the bitch live, but I rolled with yo plan. So now I need you to roll with mine."

It all hit me at the moment. He blamed me for us having to hunt Kim down. Honestly, he had every right to feel how he felt, but for him to be going through some emotional breakdown during a drill's some real hoe shit. I started to check him, but shit got real.

"This for the homie." Some nigga banged from behind us then followed with shots.

Boca! Boca! Boca! Boca!

I got low sprinting through the alley, and then I swung a left landing in the apartment, breathing hard.

The homie.

"I ain't dying by the hands of no Salem nigga?" I ran through the complex as if I'd been there before and found myself on a dark street.

A black Mazda came smashin' my way, so I ran back into the complex where I found a nigga in a Michael Myers's mask clutching something while looking around.

I walked towards the pussy.

Boca! Boca!

"Don't run now, nigga," I taunted, then gave a lil chase.

Boca! Bloaw! Bloaw! Boca!!!!

"Ugh!" The bitch nigga flew a few feet forward after receiving a back shot.

"Bitch nigga!" Flash yelled from behind me.

Anger filled my body the second I turned around and saw my bro on the ground, bleeding, clutching his heat, and coughing up blood.

"Gang, don't let me die in Salem," my nigga requested, sounding like a real Northeast nigga.

I turned around to close the bitch nigga's casket who shot my brodie.

Skirrt!

The Mazda stopped at the end of the alley, and my heart dropped as the door opened in slow motion. I did what I felt made the most sense.

I ran into the complex.

"Hey, what's that going on?" some nosy neighbor questioned.

The way blinds and doors begin opening. We must have brought the people of Salem the most action they'd seen in at least a decade.

"Come on nigga get in the car."

I ran back to the alley where I heard the voice come from and found the back door closing.

Skrrt!

The Mazda scratched off.

I noticed there hadn't been a trail of blood following the nigga we hit.

"Bitch had on a vest."

I saw Flash on the ground and relieved him of his gun, then tossed our guns in the car underneath the passenger seat.

"Nigga, we got set-"

"Don't talk. Save you energy," I demanded, pulling him up and helping him to the car.

I laid my nigga across the backseat. I hopped in the driver's seat.

"Brodie, don't go to sleep. Whatever you do, just don't fall asleep."

I smashed off as the sirens had gotten louder and floored it to the hospital, hoping my nigga made it.

Chapter 40
Freeze

I opened my eyes as wide as I'd been able to because they felt real heavy, plus my body felt sore. The room had been extra dim. I tried moving from where I'd been sitting but got nowhere.

"A snake can only slither for so long."

I looked at the nigga speaking and just knew he'd been dead, but the lil nigga survived. I stared at the bandages on his chest that covered the bullet holes.

"Lil Nuts," I chuckled, "And I see you brought company."

Three young niggas stood next to him, just looking extra hard for no reason.

"Where Trey at?" I moved my head from left to right in search of my day one loc.

"You gon' see him in a minute don't even trip cuz but on some real shit cuz love you for real." Lit Nuts taunted while his crew of flunkies cheered him on.

I sat in a chair with my arms zip-tied behind my back and my ankles zip-tied to the chair legs in a room packed with half-budded weed plants.

I'd never felt so hopeless in my life. I did a decade behind bars, came home with every intent to change my life, and got crushed after not even being on the streets for six months. Out of all the people I talked about during my bid who got out and came back two or even three times, not one of them is dead. I felt like one of them niggas on *America's Dumbest Criminals*.

"You gon' really kill a Loc, cuz?" I pulled the Crip card.

His face scrunched up as his head tilted sideways while he took a few steps forward, "How dare you disrespect my crip'n with that weak shit, cuz? Especially after how you did me."

He explained to his nigga how I left him to die when we slid on Twin and JoJo.

The hurt in his voice had been evident. I didn't know I meant that much to the lil nigga until she explained how honored he'd been to put money on my books during my bid.

"I respected you to the fullest. You knocked off a reputable Red Rag. When I found out you was gon' be in the van that day, I didn't want you or bro to do shit." He slapped his chest hella hard. "I wanted to show you how I get down."

"Save that emotional shit for Dr. Phil. Where Trey at?" I spoke with arrogance only a man determined to die could orate.

"Cuz laying right next to you," the pretty boy looking-ass nigga said.

I looked where I'd been told to look and saw my day one loc with holes all through his chest laying in his own blood with his eyes opened.

"My nigga Pretty Peet got 'em out the way," Lil Nuts pointed at the light skin nigga who told me where Trey had been. "But he died an honorable death."

"Let's get it over with. At least I'm a die by the hands of a Loc and not a brand-"

Lil Nuts started crackin' up laughing. "Cuz, you don't deserve an honorable discharge. Trey rode with you on the shit you did because you explained it after the fact. He didn't even know until about a week ago. He died because of his loyalty to you. He would never have left a loc for dead. But you ain't him, so we're gonna trade you something really valuable," he explained, then started pistol whippin' me until my screen went black.

Chapter 41
Juice

I paced back and forth in Jessie's living room, running my hands through my dreads stressed the fuck out.

"Davontae, where's my car?" Jessie asked while rolling me a blunt.

"Fuck your car, bitch! I burned it."

She sprang to her feet and started doing the most, "What the fuck you mean you burned it?"

I stopped pacing, turned around, and stepped right in her face. I gave her the coldest stare while I spoke through clenched teeth, "I said I burned it. Now is that gonna be a problem?"

She froze up then started to take a few steps back. The fright in her eyes had let me know she'd gotten my drift.

"But...how...am I going to get to work?"

"Bitch, I ain't worried about that right now. Bitch, my nigga is laid up in a hospital bed, and you worried about a punk-ass Hyundai Genesis," I spat, thinking about Flash sitting in a Hospital bed with a statewide bounty on his head.

"I never meant to get you upset, Pappi. It's just I don't like to depend on anyone but me to handle my bills and stuff."

"Jessie, that shit will get taken care of. Now twist me up a blunt so I can think." I stopped pacing and sat on the couch, and started massaging my temples.

I tried thinking who would even know to get at us in Salem, and only one name came to mind.

Ring-Ring.

My phone snapped my train of thought. I grabbed it off the table, hit talk then slapped it against my ear.

"Gang this shit out here gon' really change the game for us-"

Before Gunna called to lay all the good news on me, I had to let him know the latest.

"Flash is in the hospital, bro."

"What! Look blood. I just got this from one of my lil niggas. Check your phone."

145

Gunna had sent me a picture of D-Roc and two other nobody-ass niggas standing in front of a pool table packed with guns. The caption under the picture read, *I was runnin' to get one of these if I ran from a nigga.*

I hate when niggas try to battle the facts. It reminds me of a cop killing an innocent person on video and pretending it never happened. Lucky for mark-ass, D-Roc, most of his hoe-ass homies are gone, so when I catch him, he better have that same energy.

"Look, we can't talk too spicy on the line, so bang my line when you get back to the Town."

"What hospital bro in?"

"Downtown Salem. Get at me when y'all touch."

Jessie handed me the blunt soon as I got off the phone.

I took a long pull, just letting a cough build in my chest before releasing the smoke. There'd been so much going on, and none of it made sense. I had a gut feeling about D-Roc. Something told me we'd been followed, or they were waiting for us.

"Pappi, you wanna back massage?" Jessie asked.

Staring at her next to me low-key made me feel a lil bad for trippin' on her when she'd just been trying to help.

"Come here, sexy." I hit the weed a couple more times, then sat the blunt in the ashtray.

She laid her head in my lap and stared into my eyes for a few seconds before speaking.

"Papi, I don't wanna lose you. So, if there's any way I can help, just let me know. Even if it's just sucking your dick to take the stress off, I'm here. Ok?"

"Matter of fact, I'm a take you up on that offer." I grabbed my blunt out of the ashtray and smoked while she sucked the stress out of me.

Chapter 42
Juice

It had been a lil after one in the morning when Gunna and Mask made it back to the Town. We sat in our lil stash spot in the southeast, trying to figure it out.

"Ain't nobody heard from TJ?" Mask asked.

The question had been valid, but regardless of how I felt about TJ, I knew he wouldn't pull one of them moves on Flash. If TJ did want anybody in the gang knocked off, it wouldn't be an issue for him to get up close on any of us.

"I ain't hear shit from that nigga. But I don't see him pulling a snake move on gang," I expressed what I'd believed.

"I don't see D-Roc pushing the button on some shit that ain't gon' make him any money. And if fa sho' wasn't them Rose City suckas because Cash and Forty sitting in Salem in jail for killing Trey's baby momma-"

"Hol' up, gang. Are they in jail for the shit we did?" I just busted out laughing.

"Blood, the son pointed them out. Said it was his uncles," Gunna explained.

Honestly, I had no idea them niggas were in jail for Trey's baby momma that had me dying laughing.

"That shit crazy, but on some real shit, the homie gon' need a lawyer." I grabbed a bottle of Patron from out the cabinet and poured myself a shot.

"That's already taken care of. But if she testifies, then he could be looking at some other charges like tampering with a witness or attempted tampering. In the meantime, we need to figure out who had the drop on y'all," Mask said while breaking up some weed.

We all sat quietly for a minute just thinking, but I knew the elephant in the room's name, but I knew lil bro wouldn't pull a move like that after realizing I ain't kill Naughty, but the looks that both of my niggas shared, told me they needed my confirmation.

"Naw lil bro ain't do it." I blurted out, getting everyone's twisted thoughts of my lil nigga moving foul on me out their heads.

"I wasn't even thinking 'bout him," Gunna confessed, gaining our attention," Ray-Ray still breathing, and the way D-Roc had got done on live, in front of his bitches and everybody else could a struck a chord with Ray-Ray to the point where he felt some type of way. What happens to one fall on all."

I just slowly nodded my head, letting it all soak in because bro did bring up a valid point. For a second, I had Freeze as the top suspect, but he's the type to bounce out and run down. I thought about the Muslim niggas that had real east coast, grimy, Philly niggas accents that sounded aggressive like Dark Lo.

"Look, let's just say TJ did set it up hypothetically speaking though," Mask lit the blunt, hit it a few times, passed it to me, then continued, "What would he gain from it?" We each went up a hunnid plus just in cash off the Jaxx lash plus major work. Major to the point we had to tap in with niggas in different cities, and he's a part of that. So when one eats, we all eat. This seems something personal gang."

Ring, ring, ring...

"What's up, blood? Who this?" Gunna answered, hitting the exotic weed... "Don't play with me nigga. Facetime then and show me."

"What the fuck is that shit 'bout?" I questioned while re-lighting the blunt.

Before he could answer, the phone had rung, and he handed it straight to me.

I had no idea what to expect, but what I did see couldn't have come at a better time. The alcohol, weed, and whatever else I'd been faded out the minute my eyes had seen the bitch nigga tied down in a room filled with weed.

There wasn't shit to say after I got the location except when.

Chapter 43
Juice

My hands shook so bad I couldn't even drive. I had to let Gunna smash the Bentley. The only reason we were even in the Bentley was that the boy made it real clear that Gunna was the only one who he trusted to come with me and make sure we were in my Bentley. When we got to the house, there'd been a black Escalade truck in the driveway with some pretty boy yellow nigga leaning against it, smoking a cigarette.

Gunna parked, cut the car off, and stared at me. "Blood, I don't trust these niggas. For all I know, this could be set up. Just know if it is, we going out together." He dapped me with our Murda Gang shake.

I knew what to say, but I couldn't speak even if I wanted to. I just nodded, and together, we bounced out.

"Pretty Peet," the pretty yellow nigga introduced himself.

"Gunna."

"I know who y'all niggas is fam. Follow me."

We covered our noses the second the front door opened. Nothing could cast out the smell of death, and I just hoped it wasn't the death of the nigga I personally needed to kill as we were led into a room packed with weed plants that were mostly budded.

"You niggas call a slob to kill me, cuz?"

I looked at the nigga that I spent my life waiting to kill, tied down to a chair, beat the fuck up with his mans lying dead right next to him.

Ring, ring, ring...

"Here, homie." Pretty Peet handed me his phone.

"There's that snake nigga, but I'm a give you the chain at the same time we get the work. Don't trip off the body, my lil niggas gon' do all the cleaning. Hit me when you ready to link back up." Lil Nuts hung up.

"You know this nigga killed Top Gun, right Peet? Don't let Lil Nuts get you killed cuz putting trust in a couple of slobs. And Pretty Peet, me and yo sister's baby daddy used to go to Jumah every

Friday together when I was in the joint. It's an unforgivable sin for a Muslim to kill another Muslim, too, cuz. On Crip."

Pretty Peet waved that begging ass nigga off and walked out the room.

Normally, all the disrespectful Blood talk would have Gunna fired up, but for some reason, he found it funny. The shit had been extremely confusing watching bro crack up laughing at a bitch nigga diss'n something he solely believed in.

I just stared at the bitch nigga for a minute, taking it all in as my mind drifted back to the moment he marked himself for death.

"Juice!" my momma screamed.

I spun around and saw a nigga closing in on Juice's passenger side. The ski mask on his face and pistol in his hand let me know what time it was. I tried to scream my brother's name, but the shock wouldn't let me. Plus, it was too late.

Boom! Boom! Boom! Boom! Boom!

My mother tackled me to the floor, but my eyes never left the shooting. I saw my brother's body slump across the wheel while he ate the bullets one by one. I watched his blood spray all over the window. Then it was over. The killer hopped into the backseat of a waiting car and peeled out. My mother stopped screaming as she ran to the car.

"Oh, shit! I know this nigga is not trying to kick a prayer?" Gunna said, snappin' my stroll down memory lane.

A person's words when facing the business end of a gun always tickled me. Everyone always turns to either God or the sympathetic victim. Neither of them steered my decision. I became a faithful demon addicted to death since my nuts dropped.

A phone had sat on the floor beside Freeze. I picked it up, and to my surprise, there wasn't a lock on the phone which made shit go a lot smoother. I scrolled down the small list of contacts and stopped at the name *Aaliyah* that showed a picture of him and a young girl I figured to be his daughter.

"Cute," I held the phone to his face. "That's yo daughter?"

"Cuz, on Crip, if you-"

"You ain't in no position to make a threat," Gunna said.

"Bitch nigga, you killed my brotha in front of me and my momma. Remember that?"

He stared at me before speaking, "Whatever you got against me ain't got nothin' to do with them. I only got at you because you wanted me dead for something I did in my past life. I left all that in the joint-"

"But the first thing you do is kill my bitch while she was carrying my child. And you shot at me when I was with my daughters," I faced Gunna. "Gang, cover that nigga's mouth just in case he tries to snitch while we're on Facetime."

"Come on, man. You can't be serious. That's gon' traumatize my baby girl," he sincerely begged, sounding nothing like the person who Facetimed me wearing my brotha's chain.

After we ducked tapped his mouth, we tied our shirts over our faces and got it poppin'.

"Daddy, what's going on?" The lil girl picked up on the first ring, excited to talk to her father.

Looking at how excited the lil girl had been to see her father made me think about Lisa and Ashley. I had to block the love of my children out before my emotions spared his family's trauma.

"Mommy, I'm on Facetime with daddy."

Some fat black bitch popped up on the screen.

"Is this your husband?" I asked.

"What kind of sick games are going on?" she asked.

"This ain't a game. This is real life. Call it a favor for a favor." I gave Gunna the phone while the fat bitch covered in Muslim attire yelled threat after threat.

I waited for Gunna to position himself before doing my thang.

Boca! Boca! Boca! Boca!

"Ahhh!" the lady and daughter simultaneously screamed, piercing my ears as I continued dropping shells in Freeze's face.

Every shell I ejected in the fuck nigga's face brought a sense of peace to my mind.

"Bro, it's over. He's gone." Gunna grabbed me after I emptied the clip in Freeze.

I'd been shaking, stuck caught in shock after finally conquering a dream I've dreamed since the age of fourteen.

Gunna relieved me of my empty smoking gun then said, "Got that crab."

A bunch of screaming and crying had come from somewhere.

"You ain't hang up?" I asked after I'd regained composure.

"That's for them to deal with," Gunna replied, then we left that pussy lying next to his dead homie.

Chapter 44
Juice

The bloodstains on my Amiri jeans were very visible, but I didn't care about shit because I finally scored the bucket I'd been waiting a lifetime for. I killed faggot ass Alphonzo Harris A.K.A. Freeze. I stepped into the warehouse with two niggas I knew would squeeze without hesitation. Mask and Gunna

"You sho' these niggas ain't setting up the play for the lay-up?" Mask questioned.

I gave a shoulder shrug, "I don't know, but I do know this FN on me got thirty choppa bullets in the stick, so whatever goes down, fuck it. It is what it is."

"Sup Juice," Lil Nuts acknowledged me with a head nod as we approached him and his crew.

Outside of Lil Nuts, I had no idea who the niggas were, nor did I care. Lil Nuts had been carrying a small leather bag the size of a pouch.

He must have bro's chain in there.

"Sup gang," I greeted the lil niggas.

"Here, this you, my nigga." Lil Nuts opened the pouch, pulled out bro's custom piece, and slid it to me.

I threw it on then gave Gunna the ok. Gunna tossed him the backpack.

"That's a whole thang and ten bands for the assist," I explained

"Look, homie, I appreciate the work and shit, but we tryin' to be in business with y'all. I ain't seen the type of foreigns y'all push since O-Dawg was on the streets. We know y'all Damus-"

"I ain't a Blood or a Crip. I'm B.K C.K.," I corrected him and let him know my stance.

I noticed the fat nappy-headed nigga rubbing his hands together and smiling while nodding his head after I said that B.K C.K. shit. He didn't seem like he'd been on sneaky shit. It seemed like he might have felt the same way I felt.

"Why would we trust you after you fed yo big homie to the enemy?" Gunna asked.

Lil Nuts let out a deep sigh, then explained to us why he did what he did to Freeze and the Trey nigga.

"A dishonorable discharge," Mask smirked, then dapped Lil Nuts. "I respect that, bro."

"Look, fam, that Rose City shit is dead. Fuck all that, but I do got one last request before we go further." Lil Nuts paused for a second. "Whoever killed Top Gun gotta catch the fade with me. I'm a need that in order for us to move forward as a unit."

A fade for knocking a nigga down. I ain't even a fighting ass nigga, but if that' what comes with murking a nigga, I'll take that all day.

Mask handed me his smack, shirt, phone, and his jewelry and put the paws on that lil boy. He didn't do him greasy like kick him while he'd been on the ground, but outside of the first hit, Lil Nuts didn't land a single punch.

I noticed his lil homies looking like they wanted to try something, but they were waiting for the word from Lil Nuts. It didn't matter because neither one of them lil niggas had a hand on anything but the air. They didn't even attempt to shift their hands anywhere near the waist.

"You got heart, lil nigga," Mask dapped Lil Nuts. "Fuck it. We gon' just make y'all Murda Gang."

The looks on the other two niggas faces looked like they'd been waiting to be a part of M.G.

Gunna stepped up and spoke, "Look, you niggas found the snakes in the yard and took care of 'em, then you caught the fade with a nigga twice yo size for you brodie. Shit nigga we finna hit each of y'all with ten bands a piece for some pocket money while y'all out there feeding the streets, "Gunna pulled out his phone and said, "We 'bout to go live to let niggas know how we rockin'. The first Crip niggas to be a part of M.G.

Lil Nuts had a questionable look on his face until Gunna said the Crip part. He cleaned his face up and went to Live with Gunna.

Had I not known Gunna, I would have thought he and Lil Nuts had been rockin' for a while. I mean, like on some really in the trenches shit. When a person brings a newcomer into their family, the embrace from the top niggas means a lot, and the streets must know that you and yours are going to push the same line for anybody on the team, from the pawns all the way to the king.

Chapter 45
Juice

After all the other shit had gotten taken care of, I had some shit I had to do solo. I pushed through my city, just taking everything in floating under the dark skies in a dusty quarter-million-dollar Bentley. I loved the way Portland lit up at night. It's like Oregon's New York City.

"Our transition was crazy. We went from babies to men." Tee Grizzley spit that real through my speakers as I parked.

I grabbed the flowers off my passenger seat and made my way to my bitch. I walked through the graveyard, smiling at a few names that I'd retired, and then it hit me like a ton of bricks.

"Keisha Sanders," I said aloud. I couldn't recall a time I ever called Naughty by her real name.

I sat the flowers down, "I got that bitch nigga." I ran my fingers across her name as a joyful tear fell, "I know you see what's going on with me and Jessie. Honestly, I feel her, but something won't let me let go of you fully. I don't know if it's guilt, tears ran down my face. I wiped them with the back of my hand, "The guilt I feel for you and our child being dead…" I thought about the night she lined Marcell up for me.

I miss my Bitch.

I stood up. It felt like something came over me like an epiphany as I stared at her headstone.

"You chose that bitch ass weak nigga Jamar over a real nigga Naughty. A nigga wouldn't even shoot for you. And look where it got you." I threw the set up and my way to the only nigga I owed an explanation to.

I stepped up and touched my bro's headstone.

"Bro, I did that bitch nigga so bad, but on some real, it wasn't even just for you. I did it for me. So much has changed since you left. Momma still be giving me shit about wearing your chain. Not a day goes by where I don't think about you. I be trying to apply things in my life to how I feel you would do it." I let out a lil laugh.

"Big bro, I ain't gon' take up too much more time. I just wanted to update up how ya lil bro been down here putting' on."

It surprised me that I'd been able to make it through my whole speech without breaking down. I hopped in my car and went home to Breonna since I hadn't seen her since I'd left over a week ago.

I spent a day in the house fuckin' Bre in all three holes, and then I had to hit the spot and link up with everybody so we could put our play in motion.

TJ had been the first nigga I noticed when I stepped in the spot.

"What's up, gang?" TJ acknowledged me, dappin' me up the moment I walked in.

I couldn't remember a time when that nigga seemed happy to see me. He'd been M.I.A. for a few very important missions that really could have used his help. But before I went in on the nigga, I wanted to give him a chance to set shit straight.

"Fuck you been at nigga?" I have never been good with the passive aggression type of approach.

"What you 'pose to be my P.O. or something?" He shot back, giving me that lil cut smirk I'd been inches from wiping off a while ago.

All eyes landed on us. I looked around and saw the last four original Murda Gang niggas. Me, Gunna, TJ, and Mask. It didn't seem right without Omar and Flash around, but at least my niggas got to experience life a few levels up.

"Naw blood. Ain't nobody yo punk ass P.O., but we been going through real shit, and we really could have used you," Gunna stated, then gave TJ a quick update on what he'd missed being M.I.A. for the past three days.

"Damn, brodie, I know that felt nice." TJ dapped me with a G-Hug after hearing how I did Freeze.

"You don't even know, gang." I started emptying the guts out of a Backwood.

"Bro, I got locked up in Washington County on some old ass speeding tickets and had to sit the weekend out." He sat down and started crumbling up the runts.

It would be like him to go missing in a time of serious need. We get the drop on Kim and get in a real shoot-out that leads to Flash getting shot and locked up, but instead of me getting on some emotional shit, I pushed all my inner feelings to the side and got to what mattered.

"We gotta tap in with these lil niggas tonight so we can put shit in perspective." I started filling the Wood up with Runts.

"Gang these lil niggas really tryin' a be gang," Mask said.

"I mean who ain't tryin' a be Murda Gang," TJ dapped Gunna, "Ain't nobody did it like us since O-Dawg.

"True that. But Breeze and the Hit Squad really been up for a while." Gunna just had to involve the richest soft niggas in the town.

Hearing the name Hit-Squad got me a lil heated. It took me plotting and scheming to knock down the nigga who killed the top Hit-Squad nigga. Had I never chosen the streets, Freeze would be moving through the Town easy. It wouldn't surprise me to see Breeze in the club taking pictures with Freeze or any of them Rose City pussies.

"You always bringing up them nice ass Hit-Squad niggas. When the last time they popped anything besides poppin' bottles in a club," I lit the blunt then hit it a few times," I mean for real, though. Because as far as I remember, Murda Gang took out the whole Rose City Crips. And Breeze, Jimmy, and Marcell been in the streets way before any of us ever thought about streets." I hit the blunt then passed it to TJ.

"Why do you always feel the need to throw dirt on my relly's name?" Gunna defended his bloodline like always.

It didn't bother me one bit. To be real, it actually amused me more than anything. Gunna never liked hearing the reality of anything that had to do with Breeze being on some soft shit.

"Is it dirt if it's the truth?'

"I'm definitely checking the box that says no on that one gang," Mask added, receiving the blunt.

"Fuck all that shit! When are we meeting up with them, lil niggas?" Gunna changed the topic, cracking everybody up.

Chapter 46
Juice

Whoever didn't know about Murda Gang before we stepped in the club definitely found out when we stepped through dipped in designer from head to the rockin' custom Murda Gang pieces flooded with pure water. For some odd reason, I thought I'd have a problem being in the club Naughty stripped at, but the only thing I felt like doing' s having fun.

"Looking for a dance?" A sexy chocolate thang put her bid in.

"Yea, but we need our own section. And we need a few more that look like you," I flirted, holding five bands in one fannin' myself.

"Well, daddy, I'm one of a kind, but I can fa' show get us a couple of runner ups." She put her hand out, "I'm Ebony."

"Juice."

Her eyes lit up after hearing my name like she'd hit the Power Ball. With close to fifty thou' in jewelry on, I knew bitches would recognize a nigga as a ticket out the ghetto but never did I think a bitch a be finnin' out over a nigga.

"Oh no! You mine tonight. Let me show you to yo table nigga." She grabbed my hand and basically forced me to follow her.

"Damn, blood. Bitches out here tryin' a get choose on the gang," Gunna yelled out, being all extra as always.

It didn't even take ten minutes to get our section poppin'. We had that bitch looking like survival of the fittest. Jewelry dancing, bitches twerkin', and ones were all over the floor.

"I got all these bands on me, bands on me." I sang the hook to the Mozzy and A Boogie wit da Hoodie song that played while letting ones slide off my hand.

Mask tapped me then pointed to the entrance, "Them niggas here."

Lil Nuts and his crew stepped in looking hungry like some niggas ready for action.

I put my hands in the air, grabbing their attention, then signaled for them to pull up.

I introduced TJ to Lil Nuts' whole crew, which were made up of six niggas, including Lil Nuts, Bad News, Pretty Peet, Mugshot, Scoop, and Sleezy.

"Man, how much money is on the floor, bro?" Bad news questioned with admiration in his voice:

"This shit ain't nothing lil nigga." Gunna boasted.

I sent Ebony to get Lil Nuts whole crew bottles of The Ace. We had it lookin' like 4th of July with all the sparks flying from the bottles.

"I'd been slappin' Ebony's cheeks with a stack of cash while she bussed it to Offset and Cardi B's song *Clout* when I'd gotten rudely interrupted.

"Juice, what the fuck is going on?" Jessie spat, jumping in my face.

"Uh-un bitch, you fuckin' up my money." Ebony stepped in Jessie's face.

Jessie dismissed her with a lil hand gesture, then gave me a piece of her mind.

"You think I'm some type of weak bitch or something? My nigga ain't finna be-"

"Jessie, you know you're wrong for fuckin' yo best friend's nigga," Ebony tried antagonizing Jessie.

I'd been twisted off the Ace of Spades, really feeling myself, but I couldn't allow a cat fight to fuck off my night, so I had to finesse the situation.

I draped an arm over Jessie. "Jessie, look at me."

She turned around fast and stared straight into my eyes as if she'd blocked everything out. She didn't even look upset.

"I told you I'm going home with you tonight, right?"

"Yea, but-"

I placed a finger over her lips. "But nothin'. I ain't doing nothin' but ballin out with my bros and letting the youngin's see how we live. Ain't nobody taking yo place, sexy. Bitches know what it is. Go fix yo make-up and get yo money, girl."

She wiped her face, smiled, then gave a nigga a hug. "My bad, Pappi. I know I be trippin' sometimes, but I'm a really make it up to you tonight."

The way that thang bounced as she walked off let me know that she knows I'd been eye fuckin' that ass. Jessie's shit wasn't even the fattest in the club, but she had bitches beat in other areas. She's definitely the best in the face, and she ain't got an issue with lining a nigga up for a real nigga the bitch just needed to get her attitude in check.

"Bro, is that' you bitch?"

I turned around to find the lil nappy-headed fat nigga, Bad News, standing there with his jaw dropped over Jessie.

"According to her, I guess." I took a sip of the Ace, getting low-key irritated with the lil nigga.

I noticed a grip of strippers on the other end of the club turnin' up in somebody's section. I noticed my nigga Gunna in between a few broads, but he wasn't throwing shit. He'd been talking to somebody, but I couldn't see who it was.

Ding!

I felt my phone vibrating in my pocket.

In the lot right now, blood. The text read.

"Yo lil man goin' to the private room." Mask pointed at Lil Nuts with a thick white chick.

"I tell niggas get it how you live?" I put my phone up, sat my bottle down, went to cash in a couple of blue strips for some ones, and got my section back poppin'.

After about another thirty minutes of flexin' and shit, I got bored and was ready to fuck something. The Ace had me feelin' wavy, but the Perc 30 had me irritated as fuck, ready to slap the lil nigga Bad News for talking a bunch of bullshit in my ear.

"They section lit, bro. You think the Hit-Squad niggas got the most money in Town?

I looked at the lil nigga with a look of disgust because that's exactly how he had me feeling. I knew for a fact I wouldn't be spending a minute with him or any of them lil niggas when I walked out of the club.

"My nigga, all this ass in here, and you wanna talk to me about another nigga's money."

He must not have been used to getting checked because he had a look on his face that told me if he'd been strapped, he would of upped on me.

"This shit bunk anyway, cuz." He made my night and went to the section across from me.

I saw Jessie coming out of the dressing room looking like a real snack.

"Gang, why these niggas always sayin' we were 'posed to be Hit-Squad," Gunna popped up out of nowhere saying.

He must have been over there with the cousin he loves to save on so much. That's the only person who feels me and Gunna should have been from Hit–Squad, the nigga who ain't knocked over a soul on behalf of my big bro.

"You should a been part of a gang that don't ride for their dead homies."

"Don't start that shit blood. Shit has been Gucci all night," he whined.

"We 'bout to get up outta here anyway. Make sho' them lil niggas all leave at once."

"Shit fuck that. I'm 'bout to get me a bitch and get up out this mafucka myself gang." Gunna went to gather Lil Nuts and his people and say his goodbyes to breeze before we slid out.

"Pappi, you ready?" Jessie asked, carrying her work bag.

"Am I." I hopped off the couch and a text.

I stepped out of that hot-ass club with an arm over Jessie. I scanned the lot for anything outside the norm'. I noticed a couple of young niggas in the cut and gave 'em a head nod, and then we walked to Jessie's car. I heard feet shuffling, and off instinct, my hand shifted to my waist.

"Pappi, what?" Jessie asked after I stopped and looked behind myself, making sure I'd been in the clear.

"Naw, just thought I heard something, that's all. Come, baby, we up out of here." I lead the way.

I saluted Lil Nuts Escalade.

"Bro, I'm a get you tomorrow!" Lil Nuts yelled.

"No, you ain't," I mumbled while smiling.

Boca! Boca! Boca!

"Oh my God! Pappi move!" Jessie tried pushing me to the ground as she dove for the concrete.

Lil Nuts' frail, skinny, lil body flew against the grill of his Escalade. The other niggas tried running, but they'd gotten cornered by two niggas rockin *Scream* masks.

Boca! Boca! Boca! Boca! Boca! Boca!

"Bitch is you 'bout to have an anxiety attack or something? Get in the car."

She looked completely terrified, bundled up on the ground shivering and shit.

I kneeled down, wrapped my arms around, and whispered, "We good now. Come, baby. I'ma drive."

She slowly rose up being extra dramatic crying and shit, knowing damn well tears don't do shit to real niggas but provide entertainment to laugh about.

The sounds of sirens blaring forced me to rush her to the car, not even giving one fuck how she felt because no bitch has been worth my Freedom, ever.

Chapter 47
Juice

After Jessie finally came out of her stage of shock, being all extra and shit, I dropped twenty minutes' worth of hard dick in her and called it a night.

I got up late in the afternoon but didn't leave the crib 'till a lil after eight something. I had my phone off, and Jessie had been gone, which worked perfectly for the state of mind I'd been in lately. I thought smoking Freeze would ease my pain and allow me to focus more on my money, but as the days went by and the work began moving faster due to the fact, there'd been no real competition. The next task would be finding a plug for the type of weight my niggas and I needed. The only person off the dribble who'd be able to help is the nigga I crossed to be in the position I'm in.

I smoked some exotic weed and let my mind drift as I pulled up to JoJo's spot.

"What's up? You in this bitch dolo?" I dapped lil bro.

I couldn't remember a time I went to lil bro's crib and seen him by himself. He usually keeps his hittas with him on every move.

"Niggas out there puttin' it down for the set hittin spots tryin' a get that bag right. You know Black got people out in Salem, so bro tryin' a tap in out there and see what's good."

I nodded as I stepped in and had a seat on the couch.

Never would I knock a nigga for expanding and really trying to better his situation but for the lil nigga to even consider the thought of expanding when I'm his supplier didn't really sit right with me but instead of sounding like a hater, I humbled myself.

"Ok, lil bro tryina bust moves." I flashed a smile that matched the act I'd been playing.

"I'm tryin' a get to where you at, big bro," he walked in the room and came out with a duffle bag and dropped it on me," I never got to thank you for tossin' that assist but on some real why you just ain't kill 'em?"

"They shot at you, so it only made sense that you get to cancel Christmas for fuck niggas."

"At first, when I saw that shit on Facebook Live with Gunna talkin' 'bout the first crips from Murda Gang and blood when I say I was hot, I'm talkin' next level shit. We were 'bout to slide that second, and then I said we gon' run off on the plug."

The look I saw in his eyes reminded me of myself when I made my mind up about lashin' O-Dawg. Even though I technically didn't lash O-Dawg for it, I got his brotha. But since O-Dawg linked me and Jaxx up, Jaxx's blood was on O-Dawg's hands.

"I feel you, my nigga. So, it's a good thing I called you right after that with the play." I stood up, tossed the bag over my shoulders, dapped him, and went on about my business.

Ring, ring.

I popped the trunk, tossed the duffle bag then answered my phone.

"Yea."

"Juice, I need you to pick up Lisa from school. Rocky's gone and my car t-"

"Done." I hung up.

I had no concerns about why she wanted me to pick up my daughter from school. I loved my daughters dearly, so any chance I'd gotten to spend time with them, I took full advantage of it. The life of a real street nigga ain't promised. A nigga could die at any moment out in the field, so I cherished every second with my kids.

School had still been in session when I got there, which actually became a blessing because it saved me from the afternoon traffic.

I knew where Lisa's classroom is at, but I had to stop at the principal's office and let them know I'd be taking Lisa out of school an hour early.

"Would you like for me to call her down, sir?"

"No, thank you. I wanna surprise her. I know where her classroom is at but thank you for asking." I flashed a fake smile.

"No problem and have a nice day," the principal said.

"You too."

"I told you, boy, all you gotta do is put the work in."

"That nigga sound familiar," I mumbled after hearing a man with a deep east coast accent encourage a child.

I walked toward the door the voice had come from and peaked through the window on the classroom door and saw a tall, dark nigga with one of them Freeways beards, rockin' a Kofi teaching class. *Mr. Adulu* The tag next to the door read.

That's one of them suckas who shot at us on that night at Woodlawn Park.

I couldn't walk up and question him about it, nor could I smoke him in an elementary school in front of a group of kids but knowing where he worked helped out a lot.

Now all I had to do was put together a plan. I snapped a picture of the nigga, put my phone up, and surprised my baby girl with a pop-up visit.

Marcellus Allen

Chapter 48
Juice

After about three days of scheming, I finally found a way to get the bitch nigga who tried knocking my head off at Woodlawn Park. I started to second guess myself thinking it could have been somebody else, but after he hopped in that bulletproof joint and left the school grounds, I knew I had the right nigga. I woulda dropped him on school grounds, but there'd been too many kids around, and kids tend to remember anything that comes action-packed. Plus, I didn't wanna traumatize my lil girl. So, Gunna and I decided to run our regular pick and roll.

"That's the store blood own?" Gunna asked.

"Yea, I think that's his wife and shit," I replied from the driver's seat of a rental.

After getting the nigga's name, social media did the rest. Stupid nigga wants to be out here doing drills in the same place he runs a legal business selling Islamic oils and stuff. I guess faggot ass Alphonzo didn't tell him the type of nigga he decided to shoot at was a built-for-war and in love with funk type nigga.

"That bitch gotta fat ass blood on the gang." Gunna might be the only person I ever drilled with who has perverted thoughts during the drill.

A black Charger pulled up, and some cat bounced out, looking around, acting spooked and shit as he walked in the store Amir owned carrying a backpack.

"That nigga looks familiar," I stated, studying the boy's moves.

"That's Buckshot Bobby. He used to be a shoota for the Hit-Squad niggas. He has been on some Muslim time since bro died."

I hadn't felt the level of upset I'd reached since waiting for faggot ass Alphonzo to get out of jail. However, finding another nigga who ducked after brotha was taken from me infuriated me heavily.

We watched the bitch put the closed sign in the window, and then she led the nigga to the back while he did a few things I knew Amir wouldn't approve of.

"Bitches ain't shit she 'bout to fuck that nigga-"

"And we 'bout to bust in that bitch and wait for that fake ass Dark Lo nigga." I stated, then checked my clip.

When we got to the door started to pull it, but Gunna grabbed my arm.

"It's a bell on the door. Pull it slow."

I took a deep breath then slowly pulled the door open.

"I know you didn't just come to drop that off?" I heard the bitch say.

I held the bell while opening the door wide enough for Gunna to slide in.

"Ain't yo husband gon' be here soon?" Buckshot said.

"He's not going to be here at least another twenty minutes. And you didn't say that when I sucked yo dick in the Wal-Mart bathroom while my family was food shopping."

Gunna and I just looked at each other and shook our heads. The shit sounded like something out of a Tyler Perry movie, but the surprised guests planed on turning that bitch Quinten Tarantino gory.

We tip-toed to the back, where we walked right into it. Buckshot had his back to us while hittin ol' girl from the back.

"Oh! Stay there, you hittin' my spot," she moaned.

"What the fuck!" Buckshot yelled as Gunna snatched him out of the pussy with a neck grab and sent him to the floor.

I grabbed the bitch her hair and slammed the heat against her temple, "Where that bitch nigga Amir at?"

"I don't know an Amir," she cried with a Jamaican accent that contradicted how she sounded when she spoke to Buckshot seconds ago.

"Bitch, you think I'm stupid?"

"I'm married to mon here." She pointed at Buckshot then held her finger up, showing me her ring.

This must be how cops feel when we deny all accusations.

"We were just gon' smoke that nigga now we gon' have to catch a triple home"-

"Gunna, that nigga is on his way right now, blood," Buckshot tried pleading.

"I can't believe I fucked a snitch." She confessed, sounding disgusted with dude.

"I'm not dying for you or that nigga bitch. I can lead y'all to a whole lot of work and cash."

He now had my attention, but I couldn't talk to a nigga with his dick out, so before he explained it all to us, I decided to give him a parting gift and made a scandalous bitch on his dick while he explained.

"The backpack on that table is filled with prescription pills, and in that closet, there's a safe that holds all the cash they keep because they keep everything else in the bank-"

The bell on the door jingled, and some nigga yelled out the bitch's name.

Gunna and I both put our backs on the wall next to the door and waited. I kept my eyes on the bitch anxiously waiting for Amir to walk in.

"What the fuck is going on?" Amir barked.

Boca!

"Ah, fuck!" Amir grunted, then dropped down on one knee after I popped him in the leg.

Boca!

Gunna hit him in the back, sending him right beside the nigga fuckin his wife.

"How you gon' shoot at me and not expect retaliation, gang?" I taunted, standing over him.

"Nerd ass nigga shot up a Mosque and killed innocent people, coward. Ugh! Fuck! And I'm a kill this bitch nigga for fuckin' my wife."

I don't know how he still talked high-power shit with two guns aimed to blow him at any of heroic movement made, but I did respect the fact he didn't turn bitch when facing the business end of a gun.

"You ain't 'bout to do shit but die, bitch ass fake tough guy," Gunna said, then concluded the bitch nigga's life.

Blood splashed all over the carpet, the nigga Buckshot's face, and the bitch. The shit that shocked me was how the blood on her face or clothes didn't bother her one bit.

"I think blood fell in mouth, blood"

"Well, get ready for some more," I cut in.

Boca! Boca!!

The bitch fell forward, landing on Buckshot after I dropped two in her head and two in his.

Chapter 49
Juice

The boy Buckshot wasn't lying about what had been in that bag. Bottles of Oxys, bottles of Percs from five-milligram joints all the way up to thirty and over a hunnid bands in the safe.

"My niggas out in Washington can flip these," Gunna said, holding a bottle of Oxy '80s.

"Shit, get on it, gang. But on another, I ain't get to tell you," I stared in his eyes, so he'll understand the seriousness, "I'm proud of you."

He made a weird-ass face. "Proud of me."

"Yea, you ain't try and save yo blood homie back there." I busted out laughing in his face.

He threw a bottle of pills at me. "Bitch, that nigga ain't my homie. And that nigga did the Mase."

"The Mase," I repeated.

"Ran to God when it got hard, then jumped back in the game when he felt it was soft."

Bro nailed it for real because a lot of bitch niggas from way back did that same shit. I don't knock niggas for how they eat, but if you gon' be bangin' and the death of one of yo members don't raise the body count in yo city, you need to kill yo'self.

"You get a line on them niggas who shot at you and Flash?"

"Naw, not yet."

To be honest, I'd been more focused on the money than anything else since murking Alphonzo's faggot ass. I hadn't been on social media really. I hadn't been on any type of beefin' tip. I felt anybody who wanted me knew they had to do their homework, period.

I felt my phone dancing in my pocket and answered.

"Yea."

"Why would you tell Faith that we were fuckin?"

"Yea, why you tell Faith that y'all fuckin'?" Gunna instigated.

I started to take the phone off speaker, but I didn't have shit to hide from my nigga. I also didn't appreciate the punk bitch, Jessie, talking all crazy on my phone.

"Bitch, I don't talk to Faith."

"Yea, bitch. He don't talk to Faith," Gunna did more ad-libs, adding more fuel to a fire that I'll single-handedly have to put out.

"Nigga, you got me on speaker-"

"What the fuck did the bitch Faith say that got you beggin' to get choke slammed?"

I knew the punk bitch, Faith, still believed that I killed Naughty, but her questioning Jessie about me raised a lil suspicion. So, we listened to Jessie explain what had been said to her about me.

"Did you hear any jealousy in her tone?" Gunna asked.

"Not really. It sounded more like she was warning me, Pappi."

Damn, Mami, yo voice matched yo whole look. I'm talkin face and body," Gunna flirted.

Only one thing made sense on why Faith would even think to warn Jessie about fuckin with me, and that shit meant a lot of blood would be spilling.

"Baby, I'm a call you back," I ended the call, put my phone up, and looked at Gunna. "Faith told Breeze."

Not a word came out of his mouth, but every sentence he thought of saying showed in his facial expression.

I knew he'd been contemplating how shit would play out had he went to war against his cousin or if it would be best to leave it between me and Breeze. This shit would most likely spill over to him because if my nigga, who's also my day one, chooses to not ride with me against a group of niggas tryin' to kill me, becomes my opp.

"I think you were supposed to get lined up at the club. That nigga Breeze kept tryna get me to stay back. When I got to the door, I looked back and saw him on the phone, but I didn't think anything of it. Me and blood related, but me and you family. I chose my side the moment I found out you were lining Marcell and Jimmy, and I didn't do shit."

Hearing the words come from my nigga's mouth put me at ease with shit. For a hot second, I didn't know what to expect.

"All the chances he had to get me, why now?" I questioned.

"He loves to throw rocks and hide his hands, and he didn't want me around when it happened." I heard the hurt and anger in his voice.

I knew shit would be getting thick soon and it's gon' be a lil crazy for bro to go to war with and against a nigga he's got real love for. One thing I knew my brodie knew off the dribble without any questions ask is where my loyalty lied.

I grabbed my bread and some perc 5's for the pain that came with the lifestyle and hopped in my car as I thought back to the nigga Breeze now want' to die over

A while back...

My phone vibrated in my pocket. The screen lit the dark room up as I read the text message.

He's pullin' up now.

I stared down into the parking lot until I saw bright headlights pull into the spot right below me. I smirked behind the mask when I saw the dead man step out with a dozen roses in his hands. When he pulled his phone out while looking around the lot, that's when I knew it was time to move. I walked out the door then crept down the stairs on some ninja type of shit. I had the gauge leveled with my chest just in case he decided to head up the stairs. If he did, then they would be the last steps he climbed until he went and faced his God.

But I made it to ground level without having to pull the trigga and was my target standing in the cold with his back toward me. I crept closer as he held the phone to his ear, hoping to hear a voice I knew he'd never hear again. When he turned around and saw death up close, he did what all bitch niggas did when it was do or die time. He put his hands up and dropped his jaw.

KaBoom!

The flame jumped out the barrel and woke the whole complex.

I smirked as I turned on Finesse2Tymes and smashed off.

Marcellus Allen

Chapter 50
Juice

A few days went by without shit poppin' off. I'd been laying low at my crib by myself, and I actually like it. Bre had flown down to Texas to spend time with her grandmother. I have never been the type to question a bitch about her whereabouts and shit. I always felt whatever's gon' happen is gon' happen.

I sat in my bedroom, counting out fifty bands I planned on taking to Britt to put up for Ashley's future. I wanted to do the same for Lisa, but I didn't trust Toyah to drop it all on the child we had together and leave her son out, so I let moms handle that.

"Where that nigga TJ at?" Mask asked as we stepped out of the Nike Factory.

Gunna, Mask, TJ, and I had just hit up the Nike Factory for fresh Jay's. Gang hasn't really had time to pop it since the money has been going up. We'd been hella busy just getting shit together.

"That nigga in there poppin' at the bitch," I replied.

"I need my kicks sent to the crib blood." Gunna boasted being extra as always.

I noticed a scrapper on foes rushing towards us, knocking O-Dawg's song, *100 Shots,* the one where he remixed Young Dolph's song *100 Shots* on cue. We started nodding our heads, walking to our cars, and yelling out the hook.

"How miss he whole hunnid shots?"

The passenger's side back window dropped, and my hand instantly swung to my waist.

Empty.

"This for the homie," a familiar voice yelled.

Boca! Boca! Boca! Boca! Boca!

I got low and zig-zagged in between people trying not to get hit on the way to my car. When I got to my car, I ducked while opening the passenger door, tossed my bags in that bitch, grabbed my glizzy from under the driver seat, and did my thang.

Boca! Boca! Boca!

Skirrt!

The scrapper scratched off, leaving me standing in the middle of the street with a smoking gun.

Right then, I knew who shot Flash that night in Salem, but the drop had to be given by an inside source.

We slid to Gunna's crib so we could put our plan together. I sat on the couch across from the one that Mask and Gunna sat on deep in thought, feeding shells to a hunnid round stick.

"He really didn't care if I died," Gunna growled in a hurtful tone.

"Y'all niggas really think Breeze will do that knowing you were there? Without even giving you a chance to fix it?" TJ questioned, standing in the center of the living room, drying the blunt he just rolled.

"You actin' like you don't know what happened to Marcell or something," Mask reminded.

"Ok, but how would he know that?" TJ lit the blunt.

Mask or TJ didn't know how Gunna and I knew Breeze put the hit out on me, so I explained how we came up with that theory starting back to the date me and Flash went to smoke Kim.

"Hol' up, blood. Why we just now finding out about this?" TJ barked.

"We just put it together the other day," Gunna spat.

"I was just with them niggas the other day, blood. I coulda got smacked," TJ countered.

TJ and I had our lil disagreements here and there, but he's still gang. If someone outside Murda Gang smoked a member, the murder rate would increase by the day.

"We gon' have to go at them niggas head-on. I mean no brakes, all gas." Gunna hit the blunt then passed it to me.

"I sent Jessie to go see Flash so we can see what's the triv with bro. Plus, shit be floating through the jails fast. When she gets back, she should have a lil extra insight for us." I inhaled the smoke letting it relax my nerves before exhaling while we plotted a sucka's demise.

Chapter 51
Juice

Shit got so real in the Town. I stayed at my crib out in Vancouver for close to a month, only leaving the crib to make drop-offs and pickups. The fuck nigga Breeze turned into a whole hoe ass nigga. He blocked my whole gang on all social sites like bitches do when they niggas cheat on them. The shit cracked me up. Then we had Jimmy talking real spicy every other day on Live like he forgot I was there when them Muslim niggas dumped on us at his hood part, and all he did was hide. Instead of exposing suckas on Facebook, I exposed their insides and made their mommas cry.

Ring, ring, ring...

I grabbed my phone off the dresser.

"Yea, who this?" I answered, half-sleep.

"You snake ass nigga. I got eyes on that Bentley right now. I just wanted to say bye to yo snake ass before I reunited you with yo brotha."

I dropped the phone, snatched up my burna, slid on some shoes, and ran to the parking lot, not knowing how the fuck that nigga, Breeze, knew where I laid my head.

I stood in the parking lot shirtless in a pair of basketball shorts and Jordan 4's holding an FN with a ruler attached, looking around the lot while a light rain fell.

"Bitch nigga playing on my phone," I growled after noticing I'd been the only one in the parking lot.

When I got back to my room, I just sat on my bed, confused. I called Gunna and explained the short call I had with his bitch ass cousin.

After a few minutes of us going back and forth and coming blank, I got off the phone, hopped in the shower, and slid to bro's crib.

As soon as I made it to Gunna's spot, my phone lit up on the console.

"Fuck this bitch want?" I hit talk.

"Pappi, my car got shot up," Jessie cried.

That's when it hit me.

A Hyundai Genesis do look like a Bentley, and me and Jessie's cars are the same color.

"That shit ain't funny, Davontae. It's probably your fault why this shit happened. How could you laugh at someone trying to kill the woman carrying your son?"

My whole world stopped after hearing that I had a son on the way. I always wanted a lil nigga to carry on my legacy.

"Where you at?"

"At Poppie's off, MLK getting ready to get questioned by the cops. Pappi, I'm scared."

"Don't be. I got you. Just go home after they question you and pack up. You moving with me."

"I love you."

"Yea, that." I hung up and went to holla at Gunna to update him on the news.

"Blood, you know we gotta celebrate now. You 'bout to have a son." Gunna sounded more hyped about than I'd been about the news.

I don't know why I still get shocked by bro's over-the-top antics, but I do. Leave it to Gunna to plan a party right after hearing my baby momma got shot at while carrying my seed, and he feels now's the time to throw a party for her and me to celebrate my first son.

"Did you forget about the funk that's going on?" I reminded.

"There hasn't been a day since the moment we jumped off the porch that we weren't beefin' with somebody," he jumped to his feet and fell right into character, "I'm a smoke Breeze, get his name tatted because I still love the bitch nigga and then we gon' put him in the blunt and smoke Breeze. Feel me?"

I just stared at my nigga for a few seconds because I needed it to sink in and resonate with him. Bro says a lot of crazy shit, but I believed he really lost it at that moment.

"Blood, you looking at me like I'm not speaking what's real or something? Tell me if I'm cappin'."

"I ain't gon' sit here and debate against facts, brodie. But the way you put shit together is something else, gang." I dapped him then we smoked a blunt of runts while I waited for Jessie to hit me back.

Hearing I had a son on the way had me thinking a lil different. It had me more on my grown man shit because I had another mouth to feed. I wouldn't allow myself to sleep on beef with anyone, no matter the size of a meal, but I had to give more focus to the grind.

"You know we gon' need a new line on the work real soon, right?" I advised as I handed Gunna the roach.

"We in a different league now, and the only person I know who can really plug us, we crossed a while back." He hit the roach a few times then tried passing it to me.

"Kill it." I declined.

I didn't regret robbing Jaxx, but I did regret lining him up without having another line to cop from.

Ring ring.

Toyah. The screen read.

I held the phone up, showing Gunna who was calling me. He shook his head and smiled.

"Juice. Rocky needs to holla at you about some shit."

"Why didn't he just call?"

"Nigga, I don't know, damn. A nigga wanna help you, and you wanna be hella rude."

"I'll be there in about thirty minutes." I hung up.

The last time Rocky needed to holla at me, he gave me some important intel. Based on that, I made my way out there to see what he had to tell me that's so big he couldn't say it over the phone.

Marcellus Allen

Chapter 52
Juice

Rocky and I had been on good terms ever since I tossed him a brick of coke on the house. But when I got to his and Toyah's house, they took the dick riding to a whole other level. I mean, Toyah cooked steak and potatoes, and Rocky had been rolling up some weed with a sealed pint of Lean on the table calling my name.

"Have a seat at the table," Toyah said, sounding way nicer than she'd ever been towards me.

I wanted to chill, relax, settle in and go at things slow, but I didn't have the patience for whatever games they were playing.

"Y'all mafuckas ain't gotta try and serenade me, just ask." I got straight to it, looking from her face to his, waiting for someone to speak.

"Rocky, tell him, baby."

"I'm a be real with you. Normally, I wouldn't even come to you like this, but I need to cop a brick. I'm a lil short," he confessed.

"How short?'

"I got ten cash, and I know where Jimmy's baby momma lives. His new B.M., the one who just had his twins."

I grabbed a seat and some hot sauce to go with this steak. I looked at Rocky. "Continue."

"She stays not too far from here."

The short sentences he kept giving me had let me know he'd been waiting for me to green-light the brick of raw for ten band deal, so I just laid out my deal.

"Look, fam. Keep the ten and shoot me twenty-five, when you move the one that I'm a drop on you now."

"Ok." His eyes lit up then he gave me the address.

"I think my line might be going to the Feds, so if you can lead me in the direction, it would be very beneficial for the both of us."

Toyah sat my plate in front of me, and I demolished that shit and had her run it back one time for a real nigga.

I hadn't had a home-cooked meal in a long while, plus Toyah could cook for real. I mean the type of shit that would have a nigga coming home every night.

"I might be able to help you with finding a plug. You just gotta give me a few days to call around and see if people I know are still rockin' like that." He handed me the blunt to spark up.

Rocky and Toyah took dick riding to an all-time high. I mean, they moved like a real team feeding off of each other. Knowing how long to ride, hopping on and hopping off together. They're definitely one in the same, two peas in a pod, and perfect for each other. It really cracked me up, but at the same time, it's good Toyah found her match.

I left from Toyah and Rocky's spot and went straight to the address they'd given me by myself. I knew my niggas were going to be a lil hot that I didn't invite them to the demon's meal I'd been waiting to eat, but I figured they'd get over it.

I circled the complex, and there'd only been one way in and one way out, and that's through the black gate in front of the complex. I parked down the street from the apartments and walked through the gate as someone had been leaving. I noticed the lights that were on once when I got through the gate were now off. I sat crouched down in the bushes for so long, I caught a cramp in my thigh and had to walk it out.

The sound of a door opening snatched my attention, and out came my meal.

"Aw, how cute," I joked to myself, watching Jimmy in a tee-shirt, flip flops, and hoop shorts taking his lil wiener dog out to the bathroom.

I walked from behind, following him at a distance as he walked out the complex and stopped in the grass so the dog could piss.

I slid up on him so fast and tapped him on the shoulder, causing him to jump.

He turned around.

"Remember me?" I smirked.

He just froze with a pale face. The dog started barking, so I popped the owner.

Boca! Boca!!

Two chest shots sent Jimmy to the ground, clutching his chest, where the holes were.

I looked at the ugly, stupid good-for-nothing dog and kicked it hella hard, causing the dog to leave the owner to die.

The look in Jimmy's eyes showed the look of a nigga scared to die, but his fears did not matter one bit. He probably wished he'd never saved me that night them suckas busted on me at the store when he and his homeboy came through bussin'.

"You ready to meet Marcell?" I taunted.

It seemed as if he wanted to say something, but due to his shortage of breath, he couldn't.

Boca! Boca! Boca! Boca! Boca!

Every shot landed somewhere in his face, closing his casket for sure.

I hopped in my whip and did the dash all the way to Jessie's crib.

Chapter 53
Juice

For the past few days, Jessie had been at my crib. I had served Bre the news, and to my surprise, she took it like a G.

"Juice, you can't just be leaving me here by myself all day," Jessie complained from the bed.

She wasn't hella big, but she'd been showing for real, for real.

"I can't be sitting around here starving and shit. I got two girls and a son on the way. Plus, my son's momma likes nice things." I threw my shirt on.

"Since you put it like that, I guess I can hang out around here for a while." She sat up and leaned against the headboard. "Pappi, can you hand me the remote, please?"

I grabbed the remote off the T.V. stand and gave it to her, "I'll be back tonight early morning at the latest." I kissed her, then her belly, and got my day started.

Me, Mask, and Gunna had copped a telly to figure a few things out since TJ happens to always be missing in action when he's really needed.

"The bitch that gave Flash the line on Kim is a bitch TJ plugged Flash with." I sat quietly for a few seconds letting it all sink in.

I knew niggas would feel like I'd been trying to get TJ out the way, but facts are facts, and before I brought anything to the table, I made I had all the facts straight.

The silence that took over the room had let me know they'd been weighing out what I'd brought to the table.

"I understand TJ getting at you like that, but why Flash? And we can't just say that because of that one issue, blood," Mask challenged.

"It ain't just that though, my nigga." I got up on Mask and tapped my temple with my index finger. "Think about it. The shootin' at the Nike store, he's the only one still in the store. The shit with me and Flash and he admitted to being with-"

"He tried to backdoor you for Breeze," Gunna blurted out.

Ring, ring.

I pulled my phone out and answered on speaker.

"Good lookin' on that guap, blood," Flash said the second I accepted the call.

"That ain't no thang, gang. But look, Jessie told me that bug was inside. I got the bros here, and they need that stamp."

"Everything bro is saying about the in-house snake is green."

The look of disappointment showed all over their faces. Nobody wants to believe that one of their day ones would become a straight fuck nigga and try to line you up, but the game who chose to play can get very treacherous at times.

We chopped it up with Flash for a couple more minutes, and then we sat our play in motion.

Three deep in a tinted-out minivan waiting for a certain somebody to pull up.

"You think he gon' really fall for this one?" Mask questioned from the driver seat.

"Fa sho'. His greed's gonna get the best of him," I replied from the backseat with a Draco on my lap.

"I would hate to have to do the homie over some money we coulda made," Gunna expressed from the passenger seat.

As soon as the words left Gunna's mouth, TJ's black 550 Benz pulled up and parked. We watched him run in the stash house, leave out carrying a duffel, then the same scrapper from the Nike store shootout pulled up, and two lil niggas went in the stash spot.

"He really was planning a solo takeover," Mask said, sounding surprised.

We told TJ that Gunna and Mask were going up to Seattle to handle some business out that way, and I needed to hit up the stash house for some work, so I guess the niggas inside were left to take care of me.

I felt my phone vibrate in my pocket and pulled it out.

He pulling in now.

Ten minutes later, we were pulling up to my lil bro's spot. I spotted TJ whip in the lot when we got there. Lil bro had left the door unlocked, so we slid in real easy.

The look on TJ's face gave his snake ass away.

"I shoulda known yo dick riding ass would follow this nigga to the grave," TJ said to JoJo.

"You thought you was gon' send them weak niggas to kill me then serve my lil bro?" I said, clutching a Draco.

"How the fuck you gonna go against gang?" Gunna spat.

"Easy. We doing all this killing for what? We lined up the plug and don't even have another one. Breeze has been doing this shit for a long time, really getting to it, and ain't sat in jail one day. All by putting all that extra shit away. All you niggas wanna do is Murda-"

"We Murda Gang, nigga," Mask cut TJ's cry for help short.

I had no sympathy for a fuck-ass treason. Going against gang ain't ever been tolerated, but I wanted to make an example out of TJ's bitch ass. So, we tossed him in his trunk, smoked him, then drove his car to the park in the Hit-Squad's hood and left it there for his new homies to figure out.

Marcellus Allen

Chapter 54
Juice

For the past eight months, my life had been on the upscale. My baby mommas were no longer on bullshit, and I had a healthy baby boy who, of course, was named after a real nigga.

I had a new connect whose work was better than most, but the prices were a lil steep. However, we'd only been doing business for a few months, so I left it at that. Gunna had Seattle on smash, and Mask had Tacoma in a chokehold while I let lil bro supply the Town with my shit. All we had to do was fall back and get money.

I ain't had to bust my gun in a few months because them two lil niggas that TJ tried using to backdoor a nigga ended up going to jail on a body, and they brought Breeze with them.

"What's up with my lil Brodie?" I dapped JoJo as I stepped into his news spot.

He moved to a nice house out in Woodburn, where he planned to start a family. At least that's the story he told me.

"Tryin' a eat, blood," he responded in a sad tone.

I looked around the spot and saw it had only been us, yet he had a seat on the couch.

"You got here kind of fast blood."

"My lil side piece stay out here. That's why I always say hit me about the triv a day before, so I ain't gotta make hella trips."

"I feel that, but I need to show you something right quick." He turned on the T.V., and I couldn't believe who'd been on the screen.

My heart stung as I looked at the screen and saw the nigga who JoJo had been on Facetime with.

"Lil nigga, I gave yo everything yo ever asked for, and the second I turn around, you stab me in the back, blood," O-Dawg growled with tears falling from his eyes.

I swore to never die on my knees like a bitch, so I stood up and reminded him what caused our falling out in the first place.

"Did you forget that you took the plate off my table, nigga?" I faced JoJo and gave him a real piece of my mind, "And yo gon' side with this nigga. A nigga you don't even know. How you think Naughty a feel 'bout this?"

Naughty's name must have struck a nerve with the lil nigga because he tried a real tough act.

"Don't speak on my sister. You're the reason she's dead, bitch!"

Smack!

The right hook I gave the lil nigga dropped him on fast.

Click-Clack!

The sound of a gun cocking froze me up fast. The sounds of someone crying could be heard coming from behind.

I turned around to find Black with his gun at my temple, Ghost had Jessie's wrist zip tied with a gag in her mouth and a pistol slammed against her neck.

JoJo rose to his feet, spit blood on his own floor, then poured out his weak ass heart, "It's yo fault my sister is dead. She died over this weak ass twenty-five hunnid dolla chain you put before everything." He went to reach for my chain, and I stole on him.

Boca!

"Ah Fuck" I grunted after the bitch nigga Black popped me in the leg, sending me to the floor.

"You killed my brotha for some shit I woulda gave you. I did more for you than yo daddy ever did for you. If I didn't get caught for my last phone and had to spend them six months in the hole, nigga, you woulda been dead," O-Dawg stated.

The hurt in his eyes pained me to the core. He'd been the first person I'd crossed that really hurt me in a way I'd never felt before. I listened to him speak, and for the first time since killing Jaxx, I felt the pain I'd giving the only nigga I'd ever looked at as a big homie.

I scooted to the couch and pulled the half of blunt out of my pocket, and smoked.

"So, what's this about some Damu love," I chuckled with a mouth full of smoke. "So, you wanna kill me and my bitch for what?"

"Because a snake could only slither for so long. Yo reign is over. O-Dawg finna plug me with the work and as for the snake bitch, Jessie," JoJo looked at Ghost. "You gon' fuck my sister's best friend right after she died."

Ghost tossed Jessie on me.

Boca! Boca!

I dropped my blunt as her lifeless body lay slumped against my chest after the two shots Ghost gave her.

I knew my time had been up, but I never thought my son would have to grow up not knowing both of his parents.

The weight of a person must double after death because I really had to put a lot into moving Jessie off me.

I picked my blunt back up and continued my session. I scooted up so I could sit up straight.

"Since niggas wanna be real, I killed Twin." I hit my blunt and looked at their faces. I could tell they probably thought I'd been lying, so I broke it down for them pussies. I looked at JoJo and smirked. "Yo sister wasn't good for shit but swallowing babies. I nutted in her mouth and watched her kiss yo momma without even brushing her teeth. Since you niggas wanna compare notes, co-"

Boca! Boca! Boca! Boca!

Every shot found a home in my body, and then everything went black.

The End…

Lock Down Publications and Ca$h Presents assisted publishing packages.

BASIC PACKAGE $499
Editing
Cover Design
Formatting

UPGRADED PACKAGE $800
Typing
Editing
Cover Design
Formatting

ADVANCE PACKAGE $1,200
Typing
Editing
Cover Design
Formatting
Copyright registration
Proofreading
Upload book to Amazon

LDP SUPREME PACKAGE $1,500
Typing
Editing
Cover Design
Formatting
Copyright registration
Proofreading
Set up Amazon account
Upload book to Amazon
Advertise on LDP Amazon and Facebook page

Other services available upon request. Additional charges may apply
Lock Down Publications
P.O. Box 944
Stockbridge, GA 30281-9998

Phone # 470 303-9761

Submission Guideline

Submit the first three chapters of your completed manuscript to <u>ldpsub-missions@gmail.com</u>, subject line: Your book's title. The manuscript must be in a .doc file and sent as an attachment. Document should be in Times New Roman, double spaced and in size 12 font. Also, provide your synopsis and full contact information. If sending multiple submissions, they must each be in a separate email.

Have a story but no way to send it electronically? You can still submit to LDP/Ca$h Presents. Send in the first three chapters, written or typed, of your completed manuscript to:

LDP: Submissions Dept
Po Box 944
Stockbridge, Ga 30281

DO NOT send original manuscript. Must be a duplicate.

Provide your synopsis and a cover letter containing your full contact information.

Thanks for considering LDP and Ca$h Presents.

NEW RELEASES

A GANGSTA SAVED XMAS by MONET DRAGUN
XMAS WITH AN ATL SHOOTER by CA$H & DESTINY SKAI
CUM FOR ME by SUGAR E. WALLZ
THE BRICK MAN 3 by KING RIO
THE PLUG OF LIL MEXICO by CHRIS GREEN
THE STREETS STAINED MY SOUL 3 by MARCELLUS ALLEN

Coming Soon from Lock Down Publications/Ca$h Presents

BLOOD OF A BOSS **VI**

SHADOWS OF THE GAME II

TRAP BASTARD II

By **Askari**

LOYAL TO THE GAME **IV**

By **T.J. & Jelissa**

IF TRUE SAVAGE **VIII**

MIDNIGHT CARTEL IV

DOPE BOY MAGIC IV

CITY OF KINGZ III

NIGHTMARE ON SILENT AVE II

THE PLUG OF LIL MEXICO II

By **Chris Green**

BLAST FOR ME **III**

A SAVAGE DOPEBOY III

CUTTHROAT MAFIA III

DUFFLE BAG CARTEL VII

HEARTLESS GOON VI

By **Ghost**

A HUSTLER'S DECEIT III

KILL ZONE II

BAE BELONGS TO ME III

By **Aryanna**

KING OF THE TRAP III

By **T.J. Edwards**

GORILLAZ IN THE BAY V

3X KRAZY III

STRAIGHT BEAST MODE II

De'Kari

KINGPIN KILLAZ IV

STREET KINGS III

PAID IN BLOOD III

CARTEL KILLAZ IV

DOPE GODS III

Hood Rich

SINS OF A HUSTLA II

ASAD

RICH $AVAGE II

MONEY IN THE GRAVE II

By Martell Troublesome Bolden

YAYO V

Bred In The Game 2

S. Allen

CREAM III

By Yolanda Moore

SON OF A DOPE FIEND III

HEAVEN GOT A GHETTO II

By Renta

LOYALTY AIN'T PROMISED III

By Keith Williams

I'M NOTHING WITHOUT HIS LOVE II

SINS OF A THUG II

TO THE THUG I LOVED BEFORE II

By Monet Dragun

QUIET MONEY IV

EXTENDED CLIP III

THUG LIFE IV

By **Trai'Quan**

THE STREETS MADE ME IV

Marcellus Allen

By **Larry D. Wright**
IF YOU CROSS ME ONCE II
By **Anthony Fields**
THE STREETS WILL NEVER CLOSE II
By **K'ajji**
HARD AND RUTHLESS III
THE BILLIONAIRE BENTLEYS II
Von Diesel
KILLA KOUNTY II
By **Khufu**
MONEY GAME III
By **Smoove Dolla**
JACK BOYZ VERSUS DOPE BOYZ
By **Romell Tukes**
MURDA WAS THE CASE II
Elijah R. Freeman
THE STREETS NEVER LET GO II
By **Robert Baptiste**
AN UNFORESEEN LOVE III
By **Meesha**
KING OF THE TRENCHES II
by **GHOST & TRANAY ADAMS**

MONEY MAFIA II
LOYAL TO THE SOIL II
By **Jibril Williams**
QUEEN OF THE ZOO II
By **Black Migo**
THE BRICK MAN IV
By King Rio
VICIOUS LOYALTY II

By Kingpen

A GANGSTA'S PAIN II

By J-Blunt

CONFESSIONS OF A JACKBOY III

By Nicholas Lock

GRIMEY WAYS II

By Ray Vinci

<u>Available Now</u>

RESTRAINING ORDER **I & II**

By **CA$H & Coffee**

LOVE KNOWS NO BOUNDARIES **I II & III**

By **Coffee**

RAISED AS A GOON I, II, III & IV

BRED BY THE SLUMS I, II, III

BLAST FOR ME I & II

ROTTEN TO THE CORE I II III

A BRONX TALE I, II, III

DUFFLE BAG CARTEL I II III IV V VI

HEARTLESS GOON I II III IV V

A SAVAGE DOPEBOY I II

DRUG LORDS I II III

CUTTHROAT MAFIA I II

KING OF THE TRENCHES

By **Ghost**

LAY IT DOWN **I & II**

LAST OF A DYING BREED I II

Marcellus Allen

BLOOD STAINS OF A SHOTTA I & II III
By **Jamaica**
LOYAL TO THE GAME I II III
LIFE OF SIN I, II III
By **TJ & Jelissa**
BLOODY COMMAS I & II
SKI MASK CARTEL I II & III
KING OF NEW YORK I II,III IV V
RISE TO POWER I II III
COKE KINGS I II III IV V
BORN HEARTLESS I II III IV
KING OF THE TRAP I II
By **T.J. Edwards**
IF LOVING HIM IS WRONG... I & II
LOVE ME EVEN WHEN IT HURTS I II III
By **Jelissa**
WHEN THE STREETS CLAP BACK I & II III
THE HEART OF A SAVAGE I II III
MONEY MAFIA
LOYAL TO THE SOIL
By **Jibril Williams**
A DISTINGUISHED THUG STOLE MY HEART I II & III
LOVE SHOULDN'T HURT I II III IV
RENEGADE BOYS I II III IV
PAID IN KARMA I II III
SAVAGE STORMS I II
AN UNFORESEEN LOVE I II
By **Meesha**
A GANGSTER'S CODE I &, II III
A GANGSTER'S SYN I II III

THE SAVAGE LIFE I II III

CHAINED TO THE STREETS I II III

BLOOD ON THE MONEY I II III

A GANGSTA'S PAIN

By J-Blunt

PUSH IT TO THE LIMIT

By **Bre' Hayes**

BLOOD OF A BOSS **I, II, III, IV, V**

SHADOWS OF THE GAME

TRAP BASTARD

By **Askari**

THE STREETS BLEED MURDER **I, II & III**

THE HEART OF A GANGSTA I II& III

By **Jerry Jackson**

CUM FOR ME I II III IV V VI VII VIII

An **LDP Erotica Collaboration**

BRIDE OF A HUSTLA **I II & II**

THE FETTI GIRLS **I, II& III**

CORRUPTED BY A GANGSTA I, II III, IV

BLINDED BY HIS LOVE

THE PRICE YOU PAY FOR LOVE I, II ,III

DOPE GIRL MAGIC I II III

By **Destiny Skai**

WHEN A GOOD GIRL GOES BAD

By **Adrienne**

THE COST OF LOYALTY I II III

By Kweli

A GANGSTER'S REVENGE **I II III & IV**

THE BOSS MAN'S DAUGHTERS I II III IV V

A SAVAGE LOVE **I & II**

Marcellus Allen

BAE BELONGS TO ME I II
A HUSTLER'S DECEIT I, II, III
WHAT BAD BITCHES DO I, II, III
SOUL OF A MONSTER I II III
KILL ZONE
A DOPE BOY'S QUEEN I II III
By **Aryanna**
A KINGPIN'S AMBITON
A KINGPIN'S AMBITION **II**
I MURDER FOR THE DOUGH
By **Ambitious**
TRUE SAVAGE I II III IV V VI VII
DOPE BOY MAGIC I, II, III
MIDNIGHT CARTEL I II III
CITY OF KINGZ I II
NIGHTMARE ON SILENT AVE
THE PLUG OF LIL MEXICO II

By **Chris Green**
A DOPEBOY'S PRAYER
By **Eddie "Wolf" Lee**
THE KING CARTEL **I, II & III**
By **Frank Gresham**
THESE NIGGAS AIN'T LOYAL **I, II & III**
By **Nikki Tee**
GANGSTA SHYT **I II &III**
By **CATO**
THE ULTIMATE BETRAYAL
By **Phoenix**
BOSS'N UP **I , II & III**

By **Royal Nicole**

I LOVE YOU TO DEATH

By **Destiny J**

I RIDE FOR MY HITTA

I STILL RIDE FOR MY HITTA

By **Misty Holt**

LOVE & CHASIN' PAPER

By **Qay Crockett**

TO DIE IN VAIN

SINS OF A HUSTLA

By **ASAD**

BROOKLYN HUSTLAZ

By **Boogsy Morina**

BROOKLYN ON LOCK I & II

By **Sonovia**

GANGSTA CITY

By **Teddy Duke**

A DRUG KING AND HIS DIAMOND I & II III

A DOPEMAN'S RICHES

HER MAN, MINE'S TOO I, II

CASH MONEY HO'S

THE WIFEY I USED TO BE I II

By Nicole Goosby

TRAPHOUSE KING **I II & III**

KINGPIN KILLAZ I II III

STREET KINGS I II

PAID IN BLOOD **I II**

CARTEL KILLAZ I II III

DOPE GODS I II

By **Hood Rich**

LIPSTICK KILLAH **I, II, III**

CRIME OF PASSION I II & III

FRIEND OR FOE I II III

By **Mimi**

STEADY MOBBN' **I, II, III**

THE STREETS STAINED MY SOUL I II III

By **Marcellus Allen**

WHO SHOT YA **I, II, III**

SON OF A DOPE FIEND I II

HEAVEN GOT A GHETTO

Renta

GORILLAZ IN THE BAY **I II III IV**

TEARS OF A GANGSTA I II

3X KRAZY I II

STRAIGHT BEAST MODE

DE'KARI

TRIGGADALE I II III

MURDAROBER WAS THE CASE

Elijah R. Freeman

GOD BLESS THE TRAPPERS I, II, III

THESE SCANDALOUS STREETS I, II, III

FEAR MY GANGSTA I, II, III IV, V

THESE STREETS DON'T LOVE NOBODY I, II

BURY ME A G I, II, III, IV, V

A GANGSTA'S EMPIRE I, II, III, IV

THE DOPEMAN'S BODYGAURD I II

THE REALEST KILLAZ I II III

THE LAST OF THE OGS I II III

Tranay Adams

THE STREETS ARE CALLING

Duquie Wilson
MARRIED TO A BOSS I II III
By Destiny Skai & Chris Green
KINGZ OF THE GAME I II III IV V VI
Playa Ray
SLAUGHTER GANG I II III
RUTHLESS HEART I II III
By Willie Slaughter
FUK SHYT
By Blakk Diamond
DON'T F#CK WITH MY HEART I II
By Linnea
ADDICTED TO THE DRAMA I II III
IN THE ARM OF HIS BOSS II
By Jamila
YAYO I II III IV
A SHOOTER'S AMBITION I II
BRED IN THE GAME
By S. Allen
TRAP GOD I II III
RICH $AVAGE
MONEY IN THE GRAVE I II
By Martell Troublesome Bolden
FOREVER GANGSTA
GLOCKS ON SATIN SHEETS I II
By Adrian Dulan
TOE TAGZ I II III
LEVELS TO THIS SHYT I II
By Ah'Million
KINGPIN DREAMS I II III

Marcellus Allen

By Paper Boi Rari

CONFESSIONS OF A GANGSTA I II III IV

CONFESSIONS OF A JACKBOY I II

By Nicholas Lock

I'M NOTHING WITHOUT HIS LOVE

SINS OF A THUG

TO THE THUG I LOVED BEFORE

A GANGSTA SAVED XMAS

By Monet Dragun

CAUGHT UP IN THE LIFE I II III

THE STREETS NEVER LET GO

By Robert Baptiste

NEW TO THE GAME I II III

MONEY, MURDER & MEMORIES I II III

By **Malik D. Rice**

LIFE OF A SAVAGE I II III

A GANGSTA'S QUR'AN I II III

MURDA SEASON I II III

GANGLAND CARTEL I II III

CHI'RAQ GANGSTAS I II III

KILLERS ON ELM STREET I II III

JACK BOYZ N DA BRONX I II III

A DOPEBOY'S DREAM I II III

By **Romell Tukes**

LOYALTY AIN'T PROMISED I II

By Keith Williams

QUIET MONEY I II III

THUG LIFE I II III

EXTENDED CLIP I II

By **Trai'Quan**

210

THE STREETS MADE ME I II III

By **Larry D. Wright**

THE ULTIMATE SACRIFICE I, II, III, IV, V, VI

KHADIFI

IF YOU CROSS ME ONCE

ANGEL I II

IN THE BLINK OF AN EYE

By **Anthony Fields**

THE LIFE OF A HOOD STAR

By **Ca$h & Rashia Wilson**

THE STREETS WILL NEVER CLOSE

By **K'ajji**

CREAM I II

By **Yolanda Moore**

NIGHTMARES OF A HUSTLA I II III

By **King Dream**

CONCRETE KILLA I II

VICIOUS LOYALTY

By **Kingpen**

HARD AND RUTHLESS I II

MOB TOWN 251

THE BILLIONAIRE BENTLEYS

By **Von Diesel**

GHOST MOB

Stilloan Robinson

MOB TIES I II III IV

By **SayNoMore**

BODYMORE MURDERLAND I II III

By **Delmont Player**

FOR THE LOVE OF A BOSS

By C. D. Blue
MOBBED UP I II III IV
THE BRICK MAN I II III
By King Rio
KILLA KOUNTY
By Khufu
MONEY GAME I II
By Smoove Dolla
A GANGSTA'S KARMA I II
By FLAME
KING OF THE TRENCHES II
by **GHOST & TRANAY ADAMS**
QUEEN OF THE ZOO
By **Black Migo**
GRIMEY WAYS
By Ray Vinci
XMAS WITH AN ATL SHOOTER
By Ca$h & Destiny Skai

<u>BOOKS BY LDP'S CEO, CA$H</u>

TRUST IN NO MAN

TRUST IN NO MAN 2

TRUST IN NO MAN 3

BONDED BY BLOOD

SHORTY GOT A THUG

THUGS CRY

THUGS CRY 2

THUGS CRY 3

TRUST NO BITCH

TRUST NO BITCH 2

TRUST NO BITCH 3

TIL MY CASKET DROPS

RESTRAINING ORDER

RESTRAINING ORDER 2

IN LOVE WITH A CONVICT

LIFE OF A HOOD STAR

XMAS WITH AN ATL SHOOTER

CPSIA information can be obtained
at www.ICGtesting.com
Printed in the USA
LVHW022232210522
719400LV00013B/752